D0485315

BONFIRE MASQUERADE

NANCY DREW
girl detective®

THE HARDY BOYS
UNDERCOVER BROTHERS®

Available from Aladdin

If you purchased this book without a cover, you should be aware that
this book is stolen property. It was reported as "unsold and destroyed"
to the publisher, and neither the author nor the publisher has
received any payment for this "stripped book."

This book is a work of fiction. Any references to historical events,
real people, or real locales are used fictitiously. Other names, characters, places, and
incidents are the product of the author's imagination, and any resemblance to
actual events or locales or persons, living or dead, is entirely coincidental.

ALADDIN

An imprint of Simon & Schuster Children's Publishing Division
1230 Avenue of the Americas, New York, NY 10020
First Aladdin paperback edition July 2011
Copyright © 2011 by Simon & Schuster, Inc.
All rights reserved, including the right of reproduction in whole or in part in any form.
ALADDIN is a trademark of Simon & Schuster, Inc., and related logo is
a registered trademark of Simon & Schuster, Inc.
NANCY DREW and colophon are registered trademarks of Simon & Schuster, Inc.
NANCY DREW: GIRL DETECTIVE is a trademark of Simon & Schuster, Inc.
THE HARDY BOYS MYSTERY STORIES is a trademark of Simon & Schuster, Inc.
HARDY BOYS UNDERCOVER BROTHERS and related logo are registered
trademarks of Simon & Schuster, Inc.
For information about special discounts for bulk purchases, please contact Simon & Schuster
Special Sales at 1-866-506-1949 or business@simonandschuster.com.
The Simon & Schuster Speakers Bureau can bring authors to your live event.
For more information or to book an event contact the
Simon & Schuster Speakers Bureau at 1-866-248-3049 or
visit our website at www.simonspeakers.com.
Designed by Sammy Yuen Jr.
The text of this book was set in Meridien.
Manufactured in the United States of America 0611 OFF
2 4 6 8 10 9 7 5 3 1
Library of Congress Control Number 2010937926
ISBN 978-1-4424-0328-4
ISBN 978-1-4424-0329-1 (eBook)

KEE

GIRL DETECTIVE ®

NANCY DREW
AND THE
UNDERCOVER BROTHERS ®

HARDY BOYS
Super Mystery #5

BONFIRE MASQUERADE

CAROLYN KEENE
and
FRANKLIN W. DIXON

68767/330

Aladdin
NEW YORK LONDON TORONTO SYDNEY

CONTENTS

CHAPTER 1

SHOP TILL YOU DROP

I watched as the couple drew closer and closer to my position. They were smooth, I had to give them that. They were young and beautiful and well-dressed. They were chatting and laughing as they walked, carrying big shopping bags. They had no idea what they were in for.

This was going to be fun.

"Hi!" I said loudly as I leaped out in front of them. "Can I help you with anything?"

They both jumped a little. I was standing way too close to them, and they stepped backward. The smile on my face grew even wider.

"No thank you, uhh . . ." The woman leaned forward to read my name tag. "Nancy. No thank you, Nancy. I think we're good."

She took the man's hand. They smiled at me, clearly expecting me to move out of their way. I stayed right where I was. After an awkward moment, they tried to go around me. At the last minute, I stepped in front of them again.

"Are you sure?" I asked in my perkiest voice. "I think this dress would look really great on you."

I held up a sky blue silk dress. It was actually my favorite thing in the store—blue being my favorite color. The skirt was delicately ruched, and the neckline was trimmed in beautiful lace. It would have looked great on anyone.

The woman smiled at me again, although this time, it seemed a little forced.

"No. Thank you."

Her voice was still upbeat, but it was cold and steely now too. It was hard for me to keep from laughing.

"What about these?" I pulled a pair of men's oxblood leather shoes from off a nearby counter. "Sir?"

"Not interested," he said. He didn't even bother looking at them. He ran a nervous hand through his hair. "We're just browsing. And actually, I think the money is about to run out on our meter, and we need to be leaving. Right, honey?"

The woman nodded, and they slipped past me. Now they were moving at a quicker pace. They'd stopped laughing. The chase was on.

I tugged at the collar of my salesgirl uniform and pulled the name tag closer to my mouth.

"Bess," I whispered. "They're headed your way. They're spooked. Have fun!"

I counted to five and then walked slowly after the couple, hiding behind racks of clothes but keeping them in sight as they made their way through the store. Everything and More was River Heights's biggest, fanciest, and most expensive department store. On any given day, it had hundreds of shoppers. And today, it had two very special visitors: Shiloh and Ian Frommer, the brother-and-sister shoplifting team that had been on a two-year, multistate shoplifting spree. They often impersonated a soon-to-be-married couple, looking for things for their registry, which was the story they'd given Everything and More. It'd been estimated they'd stolen over two million dollars' worth of merchandise.

And all of that was about to end, right here, right now.

Shiloh and Ian were making a beeline for the exit that led straight to the mall parking lot. Even if they got out, it wouldn't do them much good—George had disabled their car's engine. But I doubted they were going to get out the door. Especially because they were about to walk right past the cosmetics counter.

"Hi!" yelled Bess, way too loudly, as she emerged

from behind the counter. Shiloh nearly screamed. Ian flinched. Bess smiled.

"Can I interest you in our latest fragrance? It's called Stolen."

Both Ian and Shiloh opened their mouths to say something, but before they could respond, Bess had sprayed them with perfume. From this angle, it looked as though it had gone right in their faces.

Ian inhaled sharply, and started coughing and hacking. Shiloh was frantically rubbing her eyes with her fists. Tears were streaming down their cheeks. I had to cover my mouth to keep from laughing out loud.

"I am *so* sorry," said Bess in her sweetest, fakest voice. "Here, let me help you with those."

Bess reached out to take one of the shopping bags from Ian.

"No!" he barked, setting off a fresh round of coughing. He pulled away from Bess. "We're fine."

Still unable to breathe properly, Ian and Shiloh power walked away from Bess. They were desperate now. They knew something was up.

"*Aaand* it's your turn, George," I said into my name tag mic.

I could see the hope in Shiloh's and Ian's faces as they neared the exit. It almost looked like they were going to get out. Almost.

George stepped in front of the exit, dressed in a one-piece janitor's uniform. Behind her, she pulled a mop and bucket. Whistling, she ran the mop over the tiled floor in a few quick strokes.

"Out of our way!" hissed Ian. George stepped aside politely, and Ian and Shiloh stomped right past her. Or at least, they tried to. Ian's feet flew out from underneath him, just like a cartoon character stepping on a banana. Shiloh slid and skidded, her arms windmilling, bags flying everywhere.

BAM!

She went down like a ton of bricks. They tried to get up, but neither could gain any traction. Ian began crawling away. The automatic doors opened in front of him. It looked like he was going to get away.

"I don't think so," said George. She pushed a button on her lapel mic, and the doors slammed shut.

"What is this?" said Shiloh, lifting her hand off the floor. Something shimmered on her palm. Suddenly her other hand shot out from beneath her, and her head hit the floor.

"Oops," said George. "Did I fill my bucket with oil instead of water? My bad!" She laughed.

I walked over and looked down at Shiloh and Ian trying to get up.

"Here," I said. "Let us help you."

Bess, George, and I began picking up the bags, as well as the many stolen items that had gone flying out of them when Shiloh and Ian fell. I found six MP3 players, a dozen necklaces, three expensive suede wallets, two watches—and the very same dress I had recommended!

"My, my, my," said Bess. "Quite the shopping spree you two have been on." She was holding up two purses, full of other people's stuff. Looked like they'd been practicing a little pickpocketing to go with their shoplifting.

"All right, Chief, we've got them with the merchandise," I said, leaning into my name tag microphone. Chief McGinnis was waiting for my word to send in his men.

I looked down at Shiloh and Ian, then put my hand to my chin, considering.

"You know, I have something else that I think might look great on both of you." I pulled out two pairs of handcuffs and snapped them on their wrists. "And look, they're a perfect fit!"

Bess laughed. She picked up the dress I'd shown the couple earlier. She held it against me and looked appraisingly.

"This *would* look great on you," she said. "You think they'll let us keep some stuff as a reward for a job well done?"

George and I both laughed. Bess had an eye for clothes that we could appreciate, but didn't always share.

I saw flashing blue and red lights and heard an approaching police siren. Chief McGinnis and his men were always great to have around once George, Bess, and I had solved the real problems. Before that, they usually just got in the way.

"Are these our shoplifters?" Chief McGinnis asked.

"Yup," I said. "We even gift wrapped them for you." I pointed to the handcuffs.

"Well done, girls!"

"Thanks, Chief," said Bess. She held up the dress. "Now I've got one little question for you. . . ."

Once everything was squared away with Chief McGinnis (Bess got the dress), we all hopped in my car and headed back to my place.

"Let's get some sushi!" said George as we drove. Crime fighting is hungry work, and Taste of Tokyo was right on the way. After loading up on sushi, sashimi, and miso soup, we finally made it back to my house and set up camp in the living room to talk over the details of the case.

"George, those mics were awesome!" I said. I've always admired George's tech skills.

"Yeah!" agreed Bess. "And when you remote-controlled the automatic doors closed? Priceless!" She leaped up and did a great impression of Ian Frommer slipping in the oil.

"Hello!" Dad's voice came from his office. I'd heard him on the phone when we came in. His voice was quiet and clipped, the way it was when he was working on a serious case.

"Sorry, Dad! Are we being too loud?"

"No, no. It sounds like things went well?"

"Yeah, Mr. Drew," said George. "Nancy's plan worked perfectly. Got them both, red-handed, stolen merchandise in their bags."

Dad laughed to himself. Sometimes my cases made him worry, but I knew he was proud of the work that I did.

"Look, Nancy, I've got an important case coming up. Do you remember my friend Daniel Brumfield?"

"Maybe. The name sounds familiar."

"He's a friend of mine from college, lives down in New Orleans. You met him a long time ago. Anyway, he just called me and said he needs some help. A warehouse of his was burned down, and on top of figuring out who did it, and going through the insurance paperwork, he's having a hard time deciding whether or not to sell the property."

A mysterious fire? My Spidey sense was tingling already.

Dad ran his hand through his hair. "And Hannah asked for the week off, since it's her birthday. And I don't think it's a good idea to leave you here alone—who knows what kind of trouble you might get into."

Normally I'd bristle at that remark, but I already had

an idea of what kind of trouble I was going to be getting into in New Orleans, and I was looking forward to it.

"Plus, it's Mardi Gras, so I trust you'll have a way to amuse yourself."

"Ahem." Bess stood up. Her face was very serious. "Mr. Drew, I know that you would never presume to ask George and me for such a big favor, but I want you to know that we are coming with you. To keep Nancy occupied, of course, so you can get your work done."

Dad's lips twitched into a smile. He opened his mouth, but Bess held up her hand.

"No, Mr. Drew, no need to thank us. It's simply our duty, as Nancy's friends."

"Well, I appreciate the sacrifice, girls. You really are the best." He reached into the breast pocket of his jacket and pulled out some folded papers. "I already bought you both tickets. Here are the itineraries."

"Woo-hoo!" George and Bess whooped at the same time.

"Mardi Gras, here we come!" I yelled.

CHAPTER 2

FRANK

A QUICK STUDY

For what values of x is the function
$g(x) = (\sin(x^{20}+5))^{1/3}$ continuous?

I read the problem over twice. Then a third time. I was pretty sure it was a calculus problem—mostly because it was in my calculus textbook. Aside from that, I was totally lost.

Joe and I had been on back-to-back ATAC missions for over a month now. I was so far behind in my homework, I was barely ahead of the rest of the class anymore. I stretched my legs, trying to bring some feeling back into them. I'd been sitting on a chilly Parisian park bench for over an hour, and I was all pins and needles.

"Hey, Frank." Joe's voice crackled in my earpiece.

I looked down and half covered my mouth. Though the street was mostly deserted, I didn't want anyone to see me talking into empty space.

"What's up?" I asked.

"You're doing homework, aren't you?"

"Yes," I whispered guiltily. "I've got a lot to catch up on. Why does it matter?"

"Well, because unless I'm mistaken, Sara Schulenberg just crept out of the windows you were supposed to be watching!"

I slammed my textbook shut and grabbed the night-vision binoculars from my bag. They'd pretty much blow my cover to anyone watching, but if Joe was right, it was too late to worry about that now.

I counted the windows—six up, four over. The lights were still on in Sara's hotel room. And Joe was totally wrong. Sara was standing right there, to the side of the second window, mostly hidden by the curtains . . . exactly where she was last time I looked, ten minutes ago!

I focused the binoculars more tightly. The figure was so still. Too still. It wasn't Sara, it was a mannequin. I'd been tricked.

"I—uhhh—I have a big test next week," I told Joe, trying to explain how I'd missed her. "But I undid the alarms on both her cars, and her motorcycle. And I deactivated the bombs she placed as booby traps at the entrance to the hotel garage. She won't get far."

I started shoving my things in my bag. Joe laughed into his walkie-talkie.

"Don't worry about it. I'll get her in the garage. Meet me there when you can."

At seventeen, Sara Schulenberg was the youngest, and possibly the most accomplished, jewel thief in all of Europe. She'd been known to walk into stores pretending to be royalty, or a famous rock star, and demand to try on their most expensive pieces. Once the jewels were on, she pulled out her signature pink diamond-studded pistol, tied up the employees, and disappeared onto the streets. Joe and I had been on her trail for a week, ever since she'd pulled off a daring daylight raid in Poland. We'd tracked her to this Parisian hotel, where the French police were planning a sting this very evening. But she must have gotten word somehow, and now she was on the run.

I debated heading to the garage to help Joe, or staying here in case she doubled back, when my earpiece came to life with Joe's voice.

"I forgot, what's the thing she stole?" asked Joe.

"It's called the Szczerbiec. It's the last remaining piece of the crown jewels of Poland."

"Is it by any chance a big sword?"

"Yes."

Suddenly there was a blast of static from my earpiece. I heard Joe shout.

"Joe? Joe? Nuts!"

My earpiece was dead. I grabbed my bag and took off running for the garage. Hopefully Joe would be there . . . in one piece.

I rounded the corner and leaped over the short gate that blocked off the entrance to the underground parking lot. From inside, I could hear the clang of metal against stone, and the sound of two people breathing hard. I raced down to find Joe flat on his back, with Sara standing over him. He tried to scramble to his feet, but Sara swung the sword in a vicious arc at his leg. He rolled, and the sword hit the ground. He tried to get up again, but Sara recovered quickly. She struck, coming even closer to hitting him. It was only a matter of time before she got him.

"Hey!" I yelled, hoping to distract Sara. She turned, and I ran right toward her. I lowered my shoulder and braced myself for a good old body check.

Unfortunately, I hadn't accounted for the motor oil spilled on the ground. My legs flew out from under me and I landed on my back, right at Sara's feet.

"Ha!" She laughed, an almost dainty sound. She was tiny, barely five foot two, and the sword was nearly as big as she was. But she knew how to use it. She hefted it overhead and swung it down on my stomach.

Thankfully, when I fell, my backpack had swung around, and now it was in the way. The impact hurt like crazy, and I'd have an awful bruise in the morning, but at least I was in one piece. Even better, her sword was tangled in the straps!

"Gotcha!" I yelled. I wrapped my arms around the bag and rolled to the right, wrenching the sword out of her hands.

"Joe, I've got the sword!"

As I scrambled to all fours Joe jumped to his feet and tackled Sara. They went down in a heap. And just like that, Sara went from cat burglar to captured burglar.

"I can't believe they wouldn't even let me keep the sword for, like, a day," said Joe for the hundredth time. We were back in Bayport, and Sara was behind bars. The jewels of Europe were once again safe for models and princesses.

"Well, it is one of a kind," I reminded him.

"So am I," Joe smirked.

I picked up half of my calculus textbook, which had saved me from Sara's blow and been cut in two in the process, and tossed it at Joe's head. He ducked, just as I had hoped he would. I whipped the second half of the textbook out and hit him in the shoulder.

"Ow," he said. "I never did like calculus." He rubbed his wounded shoulder.

"Come on," I said. "Let's get back to me beating you in the game, too."

I kicked a controller toward him. We were halfway through the new ZOMG Kill V, and I was determined to beat him on this one, since he had destroyed me in ZOMG Kill IV. But before we could get started, there was a knock at the door.

"Boys!" came our mother's voice. "I have great news."

I opened the door and let in my parents. They were both smiling ear to ear. And if I didn't miss my guess, Dad's grin had a bit of an extra gleam to it. I started to get that tickle in my stomach that spelled a mission.

There goes ever learning calculus, I thought. But all I said was, "Hey, Mom! Hey, Dad! What's up?"

Joe shoved the two halves of my textbook underneath the desk as our parents walked in. That would not be easy to explain to Mom, who was still in the dark about our "extracurricular" activities with ATAC. Luckily, she was too excited to notice.

"We've decided we need a family vacation. So we're heading to New Orleans for Mardi Gras!"

Mom pulled a whole bunch of shiny beaded necklaces from her purse and tossed them to us.

"All right!" yelled Joe. "This is awesome."

I couldn't help but grin. I'd always wanted to check out New Orleans. The architecture, the voodoo, the swamps, the food! This was going to be great.

"Your mother and I have already talked to your teachers about the schoolwork you're going to miss," Dad broke in on our cheering. "So you're both going to have to write a paper about New Orleans while we're there—and yes, that will require you both to spend some time at the library, doing research."

Dad winked as he said this, and I knew that tickle in my stomach was correct. We were on a mission. It wasn't often that our parents came with us, but I guess ATAC was running low on cover stories after so many missions in a row.

"To help you prepare, we got you this." Dad tossed me a DVD. It was labeled "New Orleans: City of History, City of Mystery." ATAC often hid our mission briefings in video games and DVDs, so I couldn't wait to check it out.

"Also, most of the hotels we were looking at were pretty booked up with Mardi Gras and all," Dad continued. "So we had to get rooms in two different hotels on the same block."

Joe shot me a glance. That clinched it, this was definitely a mission. Being in a separate hotel would give us enough freedom to do . . . well, whatever ATAC needed us to do. And there was no way he would have allowed it otherwise.

"We'll leave you boys to get packing," Mom said.

With that, they left. Joe had the ZOMG Kill V out and the new DVD in almost before the door was closed.

A menu screen popped up with an image of a carriage horse walking down a wide street, with beautiful old buildings on either side.

"What's this?" said Joe.

"Look at it closely," I said.

The menu options read:

> **A**rchitecture of New Orleans
> **T**he Voodoo Queens
> **A**ttractions & Festivals
> **C**ity History

"ATAC!" he shouted suddenly. He scrolled straight down the menu. After City History, he hit down again, and a new screen was revealed.

This depicted a very different New Orleans. It looked like the same street, but after a devastating fire. The main building on the street had been totally destroyed, and the ones on either side were scorched and smeared with smoke marks. There was just one option on this screen: "Mission."

Joe clicked on the button, and Vijay, our old friend and fellow ATAC agent, popped up on the screen.

"Hey, guys. Looks pretty bad, doesn't it?" He pointed behind him, to the photo of the burned street. "It gets worse." Behind him, the image changed to another burned-out building. Then another. And another. And another.

"There have been a dozen robberies in New Orleans over the course of the last year. Each has happened during one of the city's many street festivals. Witnesses say that the people responsible have been wearing carnival masks and costumes, and they look just like normal partygoers up until they start breaking windows and smashing locks."

A list of addresses and names began scrolling behind Vijay.

"The perpetrators have burned each building to the ground after robbing it, so the police haven't been able to find any clues. And nothing seems to link the different robberies. They are in every neighborhood in the city, and include rich private citizens, a hardware store, a warehouse, and a tiny deli. From some of the robberies they've probably taken home tens of thousands of dollars' worth of cash and merchandise. From others, almost nothing. It just doesn't make sense."

The screen behind Vijay changed again. This time, it showed a street full of thousands upon thousands of masked revelers.

"Mardi Gras is in less than a week. It's one of the biggest street parties in the United States. More than a million people are expected to visit New Orleans over the course of a week, for dozens of parades, parties, and general celebration. The New Orleans police are already overextended. They'll have no time to look for the gang responsible for these robberies. And there's no doubt that whoever these people are, they're gearing up for Mardi Gras as well."

The screen behind Vijay dissolved, and now he was standing in the control room of ATAC's headquarters.

"New Orleans needs help. Your mission is to find this gang, get in with them, and stop them before they strike again. You'll be on your own for this one. Any contact with the New Orleans police might give you away. Whoever these people are, they know the city, and they're going to be hard to infiltrate. Good luck."

The screen went black. The DVD stopped spinning. I turned to Joe. This was going to be a tough mission.

Joe was smiling.

"Know what this means?" he said. "Party Gras!"

Joe always knows how to look on the bright side.

CHAPTER 3

NANCY

IT'S MY PARTY AND I'LL DIE IF I WANT TO

"We are definitely not in River Heights anymore!" squeaked Bess as we got off the plane at Louis Armstrong International Airport. The airport's speaker system piped in jazz and zydeco, and the spicy smell of boiled crawfish hung in the air.

"All right, Nancy, Bess, George, listen up for a minute." We all turned to face my dad as he pulled a series of papers from his briefcase.

"These have all the pertinent information you'll need for the trip. We'll be staying on St. Ann Street, in the French Quarter, in my friend Daniel's house. He assures me he has room for all of us."

"The French Quarter." Bess sighed. "Even just the name is romantic."

"Yes, well, romantic or not, it's where we're staying. Here's a map of the area, as well as the address and phone number. I've also listed a few nearby tourist attractions—the Contemporary Arts Center, the Old U.S. Mint—and some decently priced restaurants. I trust I can leave finding the parades up to you."

This was typical Carson Drew. My dad was a lawyer through and through. He had a real talent for organization. Every vacation we went on he had a binder full of itineraries and maps. Sometimes I wish I'd inherited more of that from him.

"Thanks, Mr. Drew," said George and Bess, as they took their copies and we made our way to the taxi stand.

Dad had the taxi take a leisurely route, so we could get a view of the entire city. We glided past elegant mansions in the Garden District. They all had huge columns and big front lawns. They looked like something straight out of a movie set.

We also passed through neighborhoods that were still destroyed from Hurricane Katrina.

"After the storm," said George, reading from a guidebook, "the population of the city went down by nearly two hundred thousand people."

"No wonder so many of these houses are empty," I whispered. It gave the city a spooky feel, the way you could go from such beautiful houses to such abandoned ones.

"Look," yelled Bess suddenly, "a graveyard!"

Bess was right: We were gliding past an elegant cemetery filled with row after row of mausoleums.

"Do you know why our cemeteries look like that, why there are no gravestones?" our taxi driver chimed in from the front seat.

We all shook our heads.

"Because the river is too strong. The water is right underneath the surface, all throughout the city. Can't really bury anything. It's also why there aren't very many cellars or basements here." He drove us past the Mississippi, but it was hard to see the river because of the levees, which kept it from overflowing and blocked the view.

"We call New Orleans the Crescent City, because of the shape of the river," our driver told us. "Everything is described as being toward the river, or away from it. The river, and the shipping business that went with it, created this city."

Finally we arrived in the French Quarter. The streets here were narrow, and there were horses pulling carriages full of tourists all over the place. People seemed dressed up for no particular reason—top hats, vintage dresses, wigs.

"Are people getting ready for Mardi Gras?" I asked, when a group of people in tutus and pink wigs passed us.

Our driver laughed again. "We are always getting

ready for Mardi Gras, *chérie*. But in New Orleans, people get dressed up for the sheer joy of it all the time."

"OMG, is that a wig store across the street?" asked Bess. "I think I'm in love." I could see her planning her outfits already.

"Carson!" A shout came from the wide porch of the house in front of which we had stopped. A man in a white linen suit came bounding down the steps. He had to be Daniel Brumfield.

Within a few seconds, he had paid for our cab and was helping unload the bags. He waved off Dad's money, insisting it was his pleasure. Once the car was unloaded, he turned to us.

"And you must be the three charming young ladies Carson told me to expect. Nancy—I'd recognize you anywhere. Your mother's eyes." He put his hand to my chin and gave a wicked smile. "I always said Carson was blessed you didn't get your looks from his side of the family."

I couldn't help but laugh.

"And by the fabulous outfit I surmise this must be Bess? And George—I hear you are a whiz with computers, eh? I might have a few questions for you. But first, let's get you all settled in!"

His house was a four-story townhouse, with a beautiful and ornate black iron balcony curling around each floor. Inside it was all dark wood and slow-moving ceiling fans. The house would have felt like a model home from the 1800s, if it wasn't for the bright modern paintings that filled the walls.

"Is that a real Warhol?" George gasped, pointing at a tropically colored painting of Marilyn Monroe.

"I'll show you around the collection this evening, no worries," replied Daniel with a twinkle in his eye.

"I'm afraid, Carson," he went on, "that I lost some of my best pieces in the fire. And now I'm having terrible trouble getting the warehouse rebuilt. You know I don't believe in this stuff, but the workers say they think the site is haunted. Or cursed! I truly don't know what I'm going to do."

Daniel paused and wiped his forehead with a handkerchief.

"But we can talk about all of this later. I'm giving a pre-Mardi Gras ball tonight in your honor, and I'm sure you need time to get ready. Yvette! Come and show the girls to their suite."

An elegantly dressed older woman with short, spiky hair poked her head over the railing of the master staircase. "Order me around like that again and I'll frame your head and put it over the fireplace." She smiled at us. "Pay no attention to my brother, girls. Grab your bags and come on up. I've heard so much about you three, it's my pleasure to have you as our guests."

Yvette brought us to the top floor of the building. "Your suite awaits," she said.

She pointed to a door covered by a framed painting of a woman, which had been done in the style of an old-time comic strip.

"I think that's a for-real Lichtenstein," whispered Bess, as I opened the door. Then we all gasped in surprise.

The room behind the door couldn't have been less in keeping with the rest of the house. It looked like a Japanese cartoon. Everything was plastic, curved, and bubblegum colored.

Yvette laughed at the shock on our faces.

"Daniel and I inherited this house from our parents, but we like to think we've made our own little mark on it. Good luck finding your beds, girls. The ball begins at eight. Just in case, I took the liberty of having a few things made in your sizes. They're hanging in the closet."

Yvette shut the door behind us.

"What did she mean, good luck finding the beds?" asked George. She pointed to three large square beds against one wall. "They're right there."

I walked over and tapped on one of the beds. It was hard as a rock. Inset all along its side were thin drawers, like in a map case at a library. I pulled one open and found a purple silk evening gown that looked to be Bess's size.

"These aren't beds, they're closets!"

With a little more exploring, nothing turned out to be what it seemed. The flat-screen television hanging on one wall was really a fish tank filled with miniature octopuses, while the window on the wall across from it was really the television. The beds, however, remained resolutely hidden.

I scanned the room, thinking. An idea came to me. I walked carefully across the room until something felt different beneath my feet.

"Here they are!" The beds had been built flush with the floor, and the mattresses were customized to look just like the rug, but softer. You wouldn't know they were there until you stepped on them.

After a little more exploring, we got down to the serious work of getting ready for the evening. Thankfully, Bess was there to decode the many options and get us ready. She chose three of the simpler dresses from the many Yvette had assembled. Although each was a different color (blue for me, green for George, and purple for Bess), all three had the long, clean lines of an elegant evening gown. It was possibly the most grown-up outfit I'd ever worn.

George took one look at herself in the mirror and sighed. "This outfit basically guarantees I'm going to spill food on myself at some point tonight."

"Only eat green things," Bess advised.

Dad showed up at our door in a tuxedo, with a white

rose corsage for each of us. "Ladies, if I may escort you to the proceedings?"

Bess and George took his arms, and I walked on one side of them.

Downstairs, the entire first floor of the building had been turned into a scene straight out of a movie. There was a jazz combo playing in the corner, and dozens of well-dressed men and women glided in and out of the various rooms.

Daniel stood at the bottom of the steps, clad in a white tuxedo and top hat. On one side of him was a beautiful woman who looked like she belonged in a classic movie. She was dressed like a flapper, with short, very straight black hair, a bejeweled band around her head, and a long, fringed dress. On the other side of Daniel was one of the cutest guys I've ever seen, besides Ned Nickerson, my boyfriend. Tall, with wolf-like golden eyes, he was wearing a simple gray suit that fit him perfectly. As we watched, the woman wandered away into one of the side rooms.

"Everyone," Daniel yelled to the crowd. The musicians grew quiet. "May I present our other esteemed guests for the evening, Mr. Carson Drew and his entourage of lovely ladies, Nancy Drew, Bess Marvin, and George Fayne."

The crowd clapped politely. Daniel gestured for all of us to join him. As the crowd returned to party mode, he introduced us to the man with the wolf eyes.

"This is Aaron Pexa, one of the city's finest up-and-coming architects and real estate developers."

He shook Dad's hand, but somehow managed to have his eyes on Bess the entire time. It figured. Bess flipped her hair back behind her ear—a sure sign she thought Aaron was cute. This was going to be interesting.

"Who was that woman you were talking to before?" I asked. Something about her look intrigued me—she really knew how to stand out.

"Her name is Nicole Leveaux," Daniel said, as he craned his neck to try and find her. "I'll introduce you later. She may look silly, but don't let her fool you. She is one of the sharpest, hardest-working businesspeople in this city. She's this town's main purveyor of Mardi Gras beads, voodoo charms, and just about every other cheap souvenir you could ever not want.

"These two are both jockeying to buy my warehouse. Or at least what's left of it. Nicole wants to turn it into another of her tourist stores. And Aaron wants . . . what is it you said you wanted to do again?"

"To design the future," Aaron said, his blue eyes twinkling. "That space could become an anchor in the New Orleans skyline."

"Right, whatever that means." Daniel laughed. "But tonight is no night for business. Tonight is a night for fun. So please, girls, make yourselves at home. The crème de la crème of New Orleans is here, waiting to meet you."

At that moment, a waitress bearing a tray with three delicate champagne flutes came over.

"Sparkling cider?" She held the tray out before George, Bess, and me. We each took one.

"A toast to New Orleans," I said. We clinked glasses. And somehow, within ten seconds, we'd each been spun off to different ends of the room. Guest after guest came up and introduced themselves to me. Some asked to dance. Others told me they'd heard so much about me, the famous "girl detective" from River Heights. It was what I imagined being a celebrity must feel like.

All in all, the party was a great success, right up until the end, which came abruptly. A shriek cut over the music. The guests stopped dancing. I turned just in time to see Yvette stagger into the room.

"Daniel's been murdered!" she screamed.

CHAPTER 4

JOE

STRIKE ONE

"This is sick!" I yelled again. ATAC had really come through this time. Our hotel was the nicest place I'd ever been—and we'd been in some pretty fancy places on our ATAC missions.

We were in the penthouse suite, which turned out to have a small rooftop cabana next to a private pool! We had our own elevator up, which would come in handy in case we needed to get out in a hurry. Best of all, ATAC had hooked up the suite with some high-tech electronics. I was investigating the setup right now.

"Look, ESPN 2! In high-def!"

"Rad," replied Frank. "Now we can watch . . . what is this? Competitive foosball?"

"So some of their shows are lame. It's still objectively

awesome that we have a huge flat-screen television with every channel on Earth."

We'd been in New Orleans for about four hours, and I'd already decided it was my new favorite city. It wasn't even officially Mardi Gras yet, but there were still tons of people out in the streets in costumes. Everyone seemed to be having a great time. It was definitely the happiest place I'd ever been.

Well, aside from all those fires and everything.

"So what do we got, bro?"

Frank was sitting at one of the desks in our suite, going through the package that had been waiting for us when we arrived.

"Not much," he said. "This is a list of the twenty or so places where this gang has already struck. So far, the local police haven't found anything that connects them. Different areas of town, different owners, different kinds of places. Some of them probably didn't even have much to steal."

He pulled out a large folding map of the city and hung it on the wall. Then he took out a box of different-colored thumbtacks. He put a tack in each place that had been robbed. Then, with a tack of the matching color, he hung up the description of the location. When he was done, it looked exactly like . . . nothing. No clue there.

"Something to keep thinking about," I said. "Next."

"Honestly, there's not much else. Well, there's this."

Frank pulled a smartphone out of the box. It looked like it had been dropped—badly.

"Whose is it?"

"Some rich kid named Andrew Richelieu. Apparently, the gang stole it from him during one of the robberies downtown. He didn't even notice it was gone. The police recovered it from the crime scene and traced it to him. It's broken, and they haven't been able to recover anything from it—no prints, no voice-mail messages, no outgoing calls. I think if we try taking out the SIM card and putting it in a new phone—"

I cut Frank off. "That's totally happened to my phone before. Remember when those bank robbers shot me, and my phone stopped the bullet? Toss it here. Let me work my mo-Joe on it."

Frank picked up the phone and walked it over to me. I held it up for a second and looked at the cracked case. I weighed it in my hand.

Then I hit it as hard as I could against my other hand.

WHAP!

"Joe! What are you doing?" Frank leaped out of his chair.

"Relax, bro. Watch."

I held up the phone and hit the power button. Nothing happened. We stared at it.

"Uhh . . . ," I said. Maybe I was wrong about that whole "mo-Joe" thing.

Then, suddenly, the screen came to life.

"Ha! Score one for the Joe-ster."

"Nice job, Joe!" said Frank. He came over with a long cable.

"What's that for?" I asked.

He plugged it into the side of the phone, then pressed a button on a remote control he had in his other hand. Suddenly the screen of the phone was replicated, hundreds of times its normal size, on the television.

"Whoa. We have got to get ATAC to redo our rooms at home." This place was seriously awesome.

The phone still wasn't working 100 percent. We couldn't see the recent calls, and all the text messages looked like they were written in Swedish. But we were able to check out all of Andrew's music—a large and boring collection of the latest pop hits.

"He must just download every song that hits the Billboard charts," Frank said as we scrolled through pages of music.

We had more success with the recent videos. There was one filmed on the day Andrew's phone was stolen. Frank clicked on it, and the television filled up with a jerky, rapidly moving image.

Six or seven—or maybe eight?—people in costumes were running down the street, laughing. They all seemed to be carrying purses.

"This is weird," I mumbled.

"No, it's footage from the robbery! They broke into a women's accessories store!" Frank was excitedly pointing to one of the pieces of paper he'd hung up on the wall.

It was hard to make out much from the video. I couldn't even tell if the person holding the phone had turned on the camera on purpose. It was so jerky that they might have just accidentally bumped it. We could see the gang, but they were so covered up it was impossible to get any distinguishing marks. We couldn't even see their hair!

Then, as randomly as it started, the video clicked off.

"Look—," Frank started to say, right as the image disappeared.

"What?"

"Right there, before the video ended. I think there was a sign! Scroll back."

It was hard to get the phone to cooperate, but after a few tries, I got it to go through the video, frame by frame. Finally, in the last shot of the video, I saw what Frank had seen: a street sign in the upper right corner of the picture.

"Can you read that?" I squinted, but I couldn't make it out.

"One second." Frank pushed a few more buttons on the remote control. The image enlarged, but it was now too blurry. A few more buttons, and it sharpened again.

"Mazant!"

I pulled up the phone's map function and typed in Mazant Street, New Orleans. A map of the city filled the TV screen. Thankfully, Mazant was a small street only a few blocks long, right by the Mississippi River in a neighborhood appropriately named the Bywater.

"Looks like we've got somewhere to start," I said.

Since our goal was to go undercover and find out who these thieves were, ATAC hadn't given us a flashy car this time around. We had a pair of old, beat-up-looking bikes.

I was a bit disappointed, but they turned out to be the perfect thing for getting around the city. The streets were narrow and jammed with people getting ready for Mardi Gras. Driving would have been impossible. But the bikes made it easy to zip around the city. In no time at all, we were down in the Bywater.

It was, quite literally, on the wrong side of the tracks. We rode our bikes over them and *bump-bump-bump*ed our way into the neighborhood. It was an industrial area, although there were lots of residential streets. But there were also many big warehouses, some active, some abandoned. The streets were quieter here. After the craziness of the French Quarter, it was almost a relief.

But it was also a bit spooky. We rode past entire blocks without people. Once, a dog chased us down the street, growling and barking up a storm. Thankfully, it dropped off at the end of the block. We rode past graffiti left over from Hurricane Katrina that read LOOTERS WILL BE SHOT.

Finally we passed a coffee shop, which seemed a likely place to start our investigation. Outside were two small tables, filled nearly to overflowing with punks and hippies. Two large brown mongrel dogs lounged by the side, kin to the one that had chased us.

We pulled over a few blocks away and locked up our bikes.

"You want to do the talking, or should I?" I asked Frank.

"You can take this one," said Frank. "I'll hold the bag."

We'd worked out a plan before we left the hotel. If these guys were heading this way after one of the robberies, they either had a place out here, or they were reporting back to someone. Either way, they'd be carrying all the stolen goods, and they'd probably be looking to move them fast. That meant they needed to find somewhere to fence them. We'd check out pawn shops, too, but chances were there was someone here who dealt in stolen goods. We needed to find that person. We had a backpack filled with "stolen goods" that we'd bought in the hotel gift shop and kept the tags on. Each one had a radio transmitter on it, the size of a pinhead, which would allow us to monitor its location. We just needed to get one thing in the hands of the right person.

We walked back to the shop. As we walked inside, we listened to the people at the tables. A girl with a lip ring was talking loudly to everyone outside.

"Yeah, so then I broke his window, opened the door, and yanked him right out of the car. Tossed him on his behind. It was awesome!"

I shot Frank a glance. These were definitely the right people to talk to. We grabbed two coffees from the counter and went back out to sit on the stoop. We talked to each other for a few minutes, waiting for a lull in their conversation. Finally the chance came when the two other people at the girl's table got up. The guy on the left whistled, and the two dogs stood up and loped after him. Frank and I grabbed the seats they left behind.

"Hey," I said as we sat down. The girl eyed us with a flat, wary stare.

"What's good?" she said.

"We heard you talking earlier. Got our attention."

"Oh yeah?" Her eyes sparkled for a moment. "What y'all get into?"

"We got some stuff we're looking to sell."

I gestured to Frank, and he opened the backpack.

"It's good stuff. We boosted it this morning."

"What?!" The girl shot up in her chair. She grabbed a

laptop bag that I hadn't noticed sitting under her chair, and pulled it protectively close to her. "Dude, I was talking about ZOMG Kill Five! What is wrong with you?"

Her yelling had caught the attention of some of the other people at the coffee shop, who were starting to gather around us. Hastily, Frank zipped up the backpack and we stood up.

"Is there a problem here?" The man and woman who had been working the counter strolled out of the coffee shop. Casually—too casually—they were holding baseball bats, as though they were about to play a pickup game. I had a feeling our heads were about to be the balls!

"No, no sir," Frank started to say, but the girl cut him off.

"They're trying to sell some stolen stuff!"

This was going from bad to worse. Before the crowd totally had us hemmed in, Frank and I took off running. They started chasing us, a dozen or so people, two baseball bats, and out of nowhere, another dog.

"Get them!"

"Teach them to steal stuff in our neighborhood!"

Someone threw a rock, and I saw it bounce off Frank's backpack. This was definitely not good. I'd never really understood the phrase "angry mob" before now.

Thankfully, ATAC had trained us for this sort of situation. Frank and I split up at the first intersection. From there, it was just a matter of hopping fences, hiding behind cars, and doubling back until we had exhausted our pursuers.

And ourselves.

By the time we got back to our bikes, we were both panting, covered in sweat.

"There has to be a better way to do this," said Frank.

"I have an idea," I said. I pulled out my phone. Frank smiled when he heard the voice on the other end.

GHOST TOUR

And just like that, my vacation was officially over. With Daniel dead, I went straight into detective mode. I can't help it. Where there's a crime, there's a criminal. And catching criminals is what I do.

After Yvette's scream, the party fell into chaos. Guests were shouting. Some grabbed their things and left in a hurry. Others tried to comfort Yvette. Dad ran into the office to confirm that Daniel was dead. When he came out and placed himself in front of the door, I saw from the look on his face that it was true. I wasted no time in calling 911.

Dad kept everyone out of the office until the police came. They turned the house into a mini police station. Those guests who remained were rounded up and placed in one room. No one was allowed to leave until the cops had their names, addresses, and a brief statement. Daniel's office was taped off.

"You two all right?" I asked Bess and George, when we were finally able to get a moment alone.

"Yeah." Bess shivered. "But who could have done something like that! In his own house? It's terrible."

Across the main room, I saw my father talking to the police. I placed a finger to my lips, and quietly, we drifted over to listen in.

". . . was strangled, it looks like. Sitting in his chair. As his lawyer, do you know anyone who might have wanted him dead?"

"Well, he was in the middle of some sensitive business negotiations."

"Money." The cop sighed. "It's always money or love. We're going to need you to remain in the city until we have this figured out. I hope that won't be a problem."

The way the cop said this made it clear that he didn't care if it was a problem, Dad wouldn't be leaving.

"No, that's fine."

Dad must have caught sight of us hovering nearby, because he suddenly broke off. Bess, George, and I tried to scramble away, but we were too slow.

"Can you give me a moment, Officer? I need to speak to my daughter."

The cop waved him away.

"You girls should get to bed. This is no place for you. And besides, I'm putting you on a plane back to River Heights in the morning."

No way! I thought. Things were just getting interesting, and we hadn't even seen any of Mardi Gras. I thought fast. "The police officer said we can't leave town until the investigation is over, since we're staying in the house and all."

Dad looked frustrated for a moment, but then nodded. "All right, but I want you to leave this case to the cops."

"Relax, Dad. I promise I won't do anything I wouldn't do at home."

"That's exactly what I'm worried about." He gave a rueful little laugh. Then he grew serious. "Be careful, girls. This isn't River Heights, and the police here don't know you."

Bess, George, and I all nodded. Then we went up to our room on the top floor. As soon as we closed the door, they high-fived me.

"Fast thinking, Nance," said George. "I thought for sure your dad was going to make us leave."

"So what are you thinking?" asked Bess.

I sat down on one of the beds.

"Well, I don't know. I mean, this could be anything. Maybe someone broke in and tried to steal something, and Daniel surprised them."

George looked doubtful. "It sounds like there's a 'but' coming." She knew me well.

"*But* something tells me it's about the warehouse. The one that burned down. And judging from what Dad was saying to the cops, it sounds like that's what he thinks too. I want to find out more about the two people who wanted to buy it. Nicole and . . ."

"Aaron," Bess said. Something about the way she said his name caught my attention.

"Bess?"

"What? He seemed nice. We chatted for a while." Bess paused and looked at the ground. "And . . . maybe we have a date tomorrow."

I laughed. Of course they did. "So you got to talk to him?"

"A little."

"Do you think he could have killed Daniel?"

"I don't know! I mean, he seemed nice. A little arrogant. We only talked for, like, fifteen minutes, though, so I have no idea."

"Well, hopefully you can find out some more tomorrow. George, that puts you and me on research and Nicole."

"She seemed pretty suspicious," said George.

"Or at least totally weird," chimed in Bess.

"She was definitely a big fake. And it's interesting that she runs a bunch of voodoo shops—didn't Daniel say something about the warehouse site being cursed?"

I yawned and looked at the clock. Three a.m.! How had that happened? "Wow, it's late! All right, let's figure this all out in the morning."

My dreams were full of crazy costumes, fires, and scary music. It felt like I'd spent six hours watching a horror movie that didn't make any sense. By the time I showered and got down to eat breakfast, Dad was already gone for the day.

"Sleep well?" Bess asked at the table.

"Blargh," I responded.

"Me too," she mumbled into her cereal. Somehow she still managed to look perfect, while I was pretty sure the bags under my eyes were bigger than my suitcase.

"So what are you doing with Aaron?" I asked Bess.

"He's going to show me around the French Quarter, and then we're going to dinner. He said there's a lot of great stuff to see in the area. Don't worry, I'll listen for anything suspicious."

"I'm going to give Nicole a call now and see if she'll agree to talk to me."

I fumbled in my bag for my cell phone. Man, was I not a morning person.

I called information and got Nicole's office number.

"Hi, Nicole? This is Nancy Drew—I was at Daniel's party last night?"

"Oh, you poor girl! How are you doing? This is terrible, just terrible. My cards saw it coming, you know. I tried to warn him." Nicole sounded like a bad actress in a movie about New Orleans.

"We're all in shock here. It's been really hard. My dad, Carson Drew, is assisting Daniel's sister, Yvette, with his estate, and I said I'd help them. Do you have some time later, maybe we could talk?"

All right, it was a little bit of a lie. But only a little one! I was helping them. They just didn't know it yet.

"Oh, Nancy, I wish I could! But today is the first day of Mardi Gras season, and I'm afraid it's just impossible. But I would be honored if you took a free cemetery tour with my company, Haunted New Orleans!"

Well, I thought, *at least we'll get a chance to be near her, and maybe I can pump her for some information.*

"Thanks, Nicole, that'd be great. Can my friend George come along too?"

"Of course. And if your father would like to join us, he is *most* welcome."

The tour was set for three o'clock. We were to meet up on the corner of Esplanade and North Rampart Street.

The tour was easy to find, especially because the woman leading it was wearing an all-black Southern belle outfit, complete with a black lace parasol.

"Rats!" I muttered. The tour leader was strange—but she wasn't Nicole. "So much for that plan."

"We might as well take the tour anyway," said George. "It looks like it could be interesting."

I looked at the sun and nodded. The next thing on my sleuth agenda had to wait until after sundown, anyway.

And George was right. The tour was pretty interesting. I never knew one city could have so many freaky ghost stories! Serial killers, witches, voodoo curses, ghosts, haunted mansions—it was all to be found in New Orleans' French Quarter. But my favorite were the graveyards, which seemed to be everywhere throughout the city. They were beautiful and creepy and very Victorian.

"And here, in St. Louis Cemetery Number One," said our tour guide, "we have the tomb of the Voodoo Queen of New Orleans, Marie Laveau." Our guide's fake Southern accent was so thick that "here" sounded like "HE-ya."

The marble tomb she pointed to was small and unassuming, but there were candles and flowers all around it, and the marble itself was covered in hundreds of chalk *X*s. I was about to raise my hand and ask what they were for, but before I could, she explained.

"Many still come to ask her for favors from beyond the grave, and leave offerings, or make a mark of three *X*s."

A few of the people in our tour group laughed nervously and took photos. But the tour guide's words were scary, even if her accent was ridiculous. When a cloud suddenly slipped in front of the sun, and the graveyard went dark, even the nonbelievers hurried to leave the graveyard and get to the next site. I considered coming back with an offering, since hey, who couldn't use a little luck? But the graveyard seemed like a scary place to come alone at night.

The tour finished up right around sunset, which was perfect timing for the next part of my evening's agenda.

"Hey, George," I said, "why don't you head back to Dan—to Yvette's house and do some research on the warehouse fire, and the troubles they've been having with the reconstruction? It might give us some leads."

"Sure," said George. "I've been jonesing for some computer time, anyway. I need to catch up on my RSS feed—wait, what are you planning?"

"Nothing. I just want to explore a little bit."

George snorted. "Yeah, right. I know I can't convince you not to do what you're going to do. But be careful, Nancy!"

"Always am!" I responded.

George just snorted again. She hugged me, and we parted ways.

I walked through the streets of the French Quarter, by myself but far from alone. Every block seemed to have more people out than the entire population of River Heights! People in top hats and masks and feather boas and princess dresses and every kind of costume you could ever imagine. Above my head, parties swirled on the beautiful wrought-iron balconies that seemed to front every building in the neighborhood. It would be easy to forget what I was doing here and get swept away in the party, but I convinced myself to keep going. I had a mystery to solve!

Finally I found the block I was looking for. There, on the corner, was the burnt shell of Daniel's warehouse. It must have once been huge. Three-quarters of the building was still standing, although one end looked like it had collapsed in on itself. The windows and doors had all burst, and there were black soot streaks all over the outside. The remains took up half a block. Even this long after the fire, I could still smell smoke when I got near it.

There was police tape around the doors and windows. I did a quick look around. The street was full, but everyone was too caught up in having a good time to pay any attention to me. I chose a likely-looking door, one that had been half destroyed by the fire. On the count of three, I ducked through the entrance and shouldered the door open.

I waited for a moment in the darkness, to make sure no one came after me or shouted for me to stop. Once I was certain my entrance had gone unnoticed, I reached into my bag and pulled out a tiny but powerful headlamp. I used to make fun of George for always having a headlamp on her, but she was right—they left your hands free and made detective work that much easier. Every girl should have one.

The headlamp illuminated the remains of scraps of canvas, melted statues, and destroyed drawings. Most paints are extremely flammable, so this place must have gone up like a tinderbox. What the fire hadn't eaten, the water from the fire trucks had washed away.

"Ow!" I yelled, before I remembered I was trying to be sneaky. I'd stubbed my toe on some tools, which must have been left by the workmen.

For a second, my voice echoed throughout the building. Then it kept echoing, and I realized it wasn't my voice!

A weird wailing sound was coming from the second floor of the building. It might just have been wind, but then, it might not. . . . I looked at the stairs. They were scorched, but they were made out of concrete. They looked okay. . . .

I decided to chance it. I walked quickly but carefully, trying to step as gently as possible and stay on each stair for as little time as possible. I made it to the first landing with no problem. A smashed window provided some light from the street, and I could see the second set of steps in front of me. They looked fine.

I made it up three steps when a screeching, metal-on-stone noise began in front of me. The stairs were pulling away from the floor! I scrambled forward, but I was too late. There was no way I was going to make it to the second floor before the stairs collapsed. They were moving faster now, swaying as the supports popped out of the wall one by one.

I screamed and stepped backward. I grabbed for the railing—and it disintegrated beneath my hand. I fell.

Luckily, I hit the landing with my rear. But the struts that supported the landing were pulling out of the wall as well. I turned back to the stairs that led down to the first floor, but I could see at a glance it was no use. I'd never make it. The entire staircase was about to collapse, and take me with it!

CHAPTER 6

FRANK

WRONG SIDE OF THE TRACKS

"Whoa! Excuse me, sorry, coming through!"

I didn't think it was legal to skateboard in an airport. At the very least, it wasn't safe. Yet Lenni Wolff was doing it right now, zooming past baggage claim, ducking and weaving around disembarking passengers and skycaps loading luggage—barreling right toward us. Joe and I were about to leap out of her way when she came to a skidding halt a foot from us.

"Frank! Joe! Man, you guys travel in style." Lenni was grinning from ear to ear as she unbuckled her helmet and released her signature crazy hair. This time, it had leopard spots dyed in it. When we first met her, while working on a mystery at the Galaxy X extreme sports park, it had been bright blue and spiky.

We hadn't been sure which side she was on at first, but she'd helped us out a lot—even if she'd been causing some of the trouble we were trying to prevent. If anyone could get us in with the kind of folks who might know about the robberies down here, it was Lenni.

"First class? Last minute?" Lenni gave out a low whistle. "My ticket must have cost buckets!"

She tossed her helmet at me and picked up her board. She kept walking out of the airport, leaving Joe and me to scramble to keep up with her.

"Yeah," I said. "Well, ATAC pays for everything—"

"About that," said Lenni. "I still don't trust them. Who are they? Why they are all secretive? And how do they have so much money? Seems a little suspicious to me. You're lucky I've always wanted to see New Orleans. And it sounds like whoever these people are, they're hurting innocent people."

Lenni might not be one for rules, but she was big on protecting the underdog, which was why I knew she would come help us, regardless of how she felt about ATAC.

"People have been hurt in these fires. And everything they had was either stolen or destroyed," Joe chipped in.

Lenni's lips flattened into an angry line. "What are we waiting for?" she said. "Let's get them."

We hopped into a waiting cab and went back to the hotel. We'd had breakfast with our parents and told them we were spending the day at the National World War II Museum. We hoped Mom wouldn't decide to come looking for us.

On the way back, we briefed Lenni on what had happened so far. When we got to the part where everyone chased us, she couldn't help but laugh.

"Of course no one would talk to you! Look at you two!"

I looked at Joe. Joe looked at me. We shrugged. I thought we looked pretty good.

"You're obviously not from around here. And you scream money. Or cop. I made a few calls before I got on the plane, and I think I have a lead for you. But first, we need to get the two of you makeovers. Hey, driver!"

Our cabdriver turned his head as Lenni knocked on the glass.

"Yes?"

"Where is there a good costume store around here?"

"This is New Orleans—there are tons of them!"

"Well, take me to the best place to get some hair dye and old clothes."

That was how we ended up at Fifi Mahoney's Wig Emporium, in the French Quarter. I'd never seen that many wigs and hats and crazy bangles and beads in one place. I don't know how Lenni roped us into it, but five minutes after we walked in the door, two women were consulting on new looks for us, while Lenni perused the thrift store next door.

Three hours later we were back in our hotel room, staring at the full-length mirror in our bathroom.

"How are we going to explain this to Mom?" I asked Joe.

"Easy," he responded. "We wear hats until this mission is over. Then we shave our heads."

My hair was red. Bright red. Unnatural red. Fire engine red. And Joe? Joe's head had been shaved to the skin, except for a Mohawk rising up in the middle. We were both dressed in tight black jeans. Mine had patches covering both knees. His had been shredded at the bottom. We were both wearing threadbare old cotton T-shirts, so soft they felt like stuffed animals.

"On the plus side," I said, "if we run into Mom and Dad on the street, they'll never recognize us like this."

"Stop complaining," said Lenni. "You want to solve this case or not?" She smiled and ran her hand through my hair. "Besides, you guys look cute like this."

"So who are these people we're meeting?" I asked.

"They call themselves the Krewe de Crude. Weird name, right?"

"Actually, it makes sense," I said. "Krewes are what people in New Orleans call the different groups who get together to have floats in the Mardi Gras parade. And crude, well . . . judging from our outfits, that works too."

Joe laughed. Lenni shot me a dirty look.

"*Any*way," she continued. "I talked to some friends, and apparently, these kids are some kind of do-good, Robin Hood kind of deal. Rob from the rich, give to the poor. And New Orleans has a lot of poor people who need it. Did you know twenty percent of the city lives in poverty? It's ridiculous!"

That was Lenni, always full of righteous anger over any injustice.

"They've got a warehouse in the Bywater, which is where you guys got beat up, right?"

"We didn't get beat up," I said. "But yes, we were in the Bywater."

"Hopefully they'll know more about the scene. I doubt these are the guys we're looking for, but if we get in with them, they can give us some answers."

"So the plan is we bring them the stuff we were trying to sell, convince them we stole it from some bad corporation, and then hope they talk to us?"

"That's about it, yeah." Lenni nodded.

"I'm not sure I really like working with criminals," said Joe. "Or pretending to be criminals."

I had to agree.

"Look, sometimes you need to bend some rules.

Can't make a vegan omelet without breaking some tofu, right?"

"Gross," said Joe.

I didn't like their methods—but Lenni had a point. And besides, we needed help if we were going to find the real bad guys before they struck again. So, looking like idiots, we headed back to the Bywater.

We got more stares on the streets near our hotel, but not that many. Whether it was Mardi Gras or just New Orleans in general (or both), no one seemed to care how we looked. Once we crossed the railroad tracks that led to the Bywater, no one looked at us strangely at all—though I still felt a little nervous when we walked past that café. Thankfully, no one recognized us.

Lenni led us deeper and deeper into the Bywater, until finally we were on a street that was all ware-houses.

"This is it," she said, standing in front of a particularly abandoned-looking one. The front of it was covered in weird red scuff marks.

"Are you sure?" I asked.

"They said look for the roses."

Roses? I thought. I looked around. There was nothing growing on this street, aside from some grass in the cracks of the sidewalk. Then I realized what she was talking about.

"Oh, wow," I said. I took a step back to see better.

The scuff marks on the building? They were actually giant impressionist paintings of roses. Up close they didn't look like anything, but if you viewed the building from across the street, they were beautiful.

Lenni knocked on the door.

"It's open!" someone yelled from inside. I was shocked. They left their door unlocked? In this neighborhood?

But once we got inside, I understood why. There had to be a dozen people lounging around inside a huge open space. There were couches and rugs and dogs, strange sculptures made of bits of mannequins and feathers hanging from the ceiling. There were plants everywhere, giant vines crisscrossing the space, soaking in the sun that came through the many windows and a partially destroyed roof. The place looked like a cross between a Salvador Dali painting and a junk shop.

"Is Sybil around?"

A voice called out from the couch, "Who dat?"

"It's Lenni. Sharkey told me to get in touch with you?"

"Come on over," the voice yelled.

Sybil turned out to be a very young-looking girl in a retro sundress. If it hadn't been for the flower tattoos that covered her arms and legs, I would have guessed she was fifteen.

Lenni laid out the cover story we had devised. The three of us were in town, hitchhiking across the United

States. We had some stuff we came across along the way—"dropped off the back of a truck," was the way Lenni put it. We'd heard they were the people to get in touch with.

"You think we can help you out?" said Sybil.

"That's what Sharkey told me," said Lenni.

Sybil turned on Joe.

"So the three of you just show up, waltz into my house, and accuse me of dealing in stolen stuff? Are you trying to insult me?"

People were beginning to drift over, as Sybil's voice got louder and louder.

"No!" I broke in. This was not going the way we'd intended. "We're not—not trying to insult you. We're just—we—"

I was about to apologize and try to get us out of there, when Lenni cut me off.

"All's I know is I asked who were the major operators in this town, and your name kept coming up."

Sybil had been sitting on the couch, but she leaped up at that. She and Lenni were suddenly standing toe to toe.

"You accusing me of something? Just come out and say it!"

Lenni opened her mouth, but instead of saying anything, she pushed Sybil. Sybil stumbled backward—and then jumped on Lenni. Lenni teetered for a second, and then fell over on top of Sybil. They started twisting and wrestling on the ground. The other assembled people in the warehouse started howling and rushing us. Someone slammed into my back. I stumbled into someone else, who shoved me violently into Joe.

Two seconds later, we were in the middle of an all-out brawl.

CHAPTER 7

NANCY

THE FIRE SPREADS

The stairs had collapsed to the ground. The landing I was on was tilting and shuddering as one by one the struts that held it up pulled out of the wall. I looked down: The floor was a good twenty feet below, and strewn with broken glass, bits of metal, and debris. If the fall didn't kill me, tetanus would.

There was a horrible screeching sound as the metal of the last struts pulled out of the wall. This was it. I closed my eyes. I couldn't help myself—I screamed.

Something slammed into my chest. The air was knocked out of my lungs. I felt myself flying through the air. I braced myself, knowing there was nothing I could do to stop myself from hitting the ground, hard.

But it didn't happen. I landed on something only a

few feet away. I heard the booming sound of the stair-well landing hitting the ground below. Whatever had hit my chest had held me up. I opened my eyes to find myself twenty feet up in the air, on the branch of a big old oak tree, staring into Bess's face.

"Bess?"

"Oh, Nancy! Thank God we got here in time."

I looked down. The thing that had hit my chest was an arm—Aaron Pexa's arm, to be exact. He must have yanked me right out the window. I grabbed the trunk of the tree, and he let go.

"Thank you! If you hadn't come along, I don't know what I would have done." A thought occurred to me. "How did you guys end up in this tree, anyway?"

"Aaron and I went out to dinner in the French Quar-ter, and afterward, he wanted to tell me about his plans for his next building. It's going to be here, if he can buy the lot now that Daniel is . . . you know."

"It's going to be the gem of New Orleans," said Aaron, breaking in. "It will be a boutique hotel, which will look just like a traditional New Orleans mansion, but the facade will be cast entirely from glass, a perfect blending of the modern and the traditional."

"We were standing outside," Bess continued, "and Aaron was describing it all to me, when we first heard the noise. Then you screamed, and I knew you were in there! I was about to run in, when Aaron started climbing the tree—since the scream had come from above us and all. What happened?"

I told them about the strange noises and the collapsing staircase. "If it wasn't for your quick thinking, Aaron, I think Bess and I would both be dead—me from falling, and Bess because I landed on her!"

"What were you doing in there?" asked Aaron. Was it the adrenaline from my near-death experience, or was there something weird in his tone?

"Nothing—I went for a walk after the graveyard tour George and I took, and I heard a weird noise coming from inside. I thought someone was crying or something. The next thing I realized, the stairs were collapsing. I didn't even know it was Daniel's warehouse!"

Bess shot me a look. She knew it wasn't the full truth. But even though Aaron had saved me, I still didn't know for sure if I could trust him. And besides, it was close enough to the truth.

"You should be more careful before running off into strange buildings, Ms. Drew."

Now he was beginning to sound like my dad. Or worse—Chief McGinnis.

"Let me help you down." Aaron offered me his arm. Instead, I grabbed the branch below my feet and swung down, then wrapped my legs around the tree and shimmied to the ground. The day I needed help to get out of a tree would be the day they took away my girl detective card!

Aaron and Bess slowly made their way down behind me. While they descended, I spotted a pay phone across the street and ran over to make a call—one I didn't want recorded on my cell phone.

"Hi, 911? I was just walking down the street and I heard a crash from inside this burned-down building— I think something big fell!" I gave the address and quickly hung up before they asked for my name. Some-one needed to check the rest of the building out before workmen came in the morning. I would feel terrible if something else collapsed and hurt somebody.

Aaron insisted on walking Bess and me home. I didn't mind, really. They mostly chatted with each other, and it gave me some time to think about what had just happened.

What was that voice I'd heard? No one else came running when the stairs collapsed. Perhaps they'd stayed upstairs. Or there may have been another exit to the roof—but most of the roof had been destroyed. Maybe it was the Haunted New Orleans tour I had just been on. Maybe it was the weird shadows that played off the flickering gas lamps on the streets. Maybe it was just some residual fear from nearly falling to my death. But the hair on the back of my neck began to prickle. Daniel had mentioned something about the construction site being cursed. This was New Orleans, city of voodoo, after all. What if what I'd heard . . . wasn't a person at all?

"Hello, Earth to Nancy?"

I shook my head hard, to dispel the creepy horror-movie thoughts that had taken over. Somehow, without my noticing, we'd walked all the way back to what had been Daniel's house. I tried to recall the conversation, but I couldn't remember what anyone had said.

"I'm sorry, what did you say, Bess?"

"Aaron was wondering if we wanted to come with him to the ball his friend Andrew is hosting tomorrow."

I thought about it for a second. What I really wanted to be doing was some more investigating . . . but Aaron was a suspect.

"Maybe," I hedged. "After tonight, I'm not sure how much I'll be up for."

"Totally understandable, Ms. Drew," said Aaron. "Too much excitement can be a dangerous thing. I myself must head home and get some sleep. I've got another busy day ahead of me tomorrow, designing the future."

With that, Aaron said good-bye to us. I couldn't help but notice that he took Bess's hand and kissed it. Bess had a way with the guys. After that, he turned and strode purposefully off into the night.

"Spill it," I said to Bess as we walked inside.

"Yeah," said George, who must have been waiting

up for us. "I want to hear all about the date. Did you end up their third wheel, Nance?"

"Only by accident," I responded.

"And boy, does she mean accident!" said Bess.

George gave me a quizzical look. I explained about the warehouse, and the collapsing staircase, and Aaron's last-minute rescue.

"Nancy! Can't leave you alone for one minute. Did you at least find anything out?"

"No." I paused. "Well, maybe. There was this weird sound, like a voice, crying from the second floor. I don't know what it was."

"You don't think it's actually haunted, do you?" said Bess.

"Of course not!" I snapped. "Ghosts don't exist. Right?"

"Yeah," agreed George. "There are lots of explanations. Weird echoes. Cats. Daniel said the workers think the place is haunted—maybe someone is trying to sabotage the construction. It's pretty easy to make voices appear somewhere using a radio transmitter, like what we used to communicate on that shoplifting case."

"Did you guys talk to Nicole, the resident voodoo expert? I wonder if she knows more about this haunting than she's telling."

I told her how we'd failed to meet up with her but would try again. Then it was Bess's turn to tell us about her night.

"It was nice. Aaron's sweet! And so handsome. He's a little egotistical, though. If I had to look at one more drawing of his 'New Orleans, City of the Future,' I would have fallen asleep."

"Do you think he could have killed Daniel?"

"I don't know," said Bess. "We only hung out for a few hours. He seemed genuinely sad that Daniel was dead. But who knows? If there's one thing that being friends with you has taught me, Nancy, it's that anyone can be the bad guy."

"Well, while the two of you were out getting nothing done," said George, "I did a little research, and struck gold. Take a look at this."

She handed each of us a printout of a newspaper article from the *Times-Picayune*. I scanned it quickly. Warehouse . . . robbed . . . burned to the ground.

"So, it's another article about the arson at Daniel's warehouse?" asked Bess.

"Nope, that's the thing. Look at the date."

I looked at the header on the page.

"This was a full year ago!" I said.

"Yup. Now look at these."

George handed me a dozen more printouts. Each was a newspaper article about a dual robbery/arson, all in New Orleans in the last year and a half. In each one, the MO was exactly the same: The buildings were robbed, and then burned to the ground to hide the evidence. In the ones where there were witnesses, they all reported seeing a gang of costumed young people running from the scene. The police had no leads.

"Is there anything that connects all these places?" I asked, excited. Now we were getting somewhere!

"None that I've been able to find," George answered. "They're all over the city. Some are rich, some are poor. Some are businesses, some are homes. It seems completely random. They don't even usually seem to get that much from the places they rob."

"So they're doing it for the kicks?" said Bess. "A group of kids out to have some adventure, whatever the cost to other people?"

"Maybe," I said. "But then why kill Daniel? That doesn't make sense."

We all read through the articles quietly, absorbing the facts that were changing the case we thought we were on. Whoever these people were, they were smart. By striking only during festival times, they gave themselves a cover for wearing costumes, crowds to disappear into, and blocks full of revelers who prevented police or fire trucks from getting to the scene of their crimes until it was too late.

"What if . . ." I paused. The idea was not a happy thought.

"What, Nance?" prompted George.

"What if we're looking at two different crimes? What

if the people who burned down Daniel's warehouse didn't kill him? Or what if someone burned down his warehouse to make it look like it was part of this crime spree, and really they were just after him?"

"So either we're looking for a gang of arsonists, and a murderer . . . ," said Bess.

"Or a gang of arsonists who are also murderers . . . ," added George.

"Or a single murderer-slash-arsonist pretending to be a gang of arsonists in order to cover his or her tracks," I finished.

CHAPTER 8

JOE

REAL PARTY KILLERS

I saw Lenni go down in a heap, with Sybil on top of her. A guy with biceps the size of my head threw a devastating punch right at Frank's head. Thankfully, Frank managed to duck just in time, and with a careful push, sent the guy tumbling. A second later, someone grabbed me from behind and sent me flying into a couch. After that, the room was just a mass of arms and legs, screaming and yelling.

I managed to lock my legs around the person on top of me, and I flipped him over onto the ground. Lenni was on her feet again, locked arm in arm with Sybil. Another girl was sneaking up behind her, though, about to knock her on the head. With nothing else to do, I yanked one of the pillows off the couch and threw it at her. I managed to clock her in the head, which probably didn't hurt her all that much, but did slow her down long enough for Lenni to toss Sybil into her.

"Bull's-eye!" Lenni yelled, before leaping back on top of Sybil.

Frank was being circled by three punks who took turns darting in and throwing punches at him. So far none of them had managed to land, but once they did, he'd be in trouble. I made my way over to him, hopping over a writhing mass of people on the ground. Somehow, this no longer seemed to be about us—the Krewe de Crude was fighting with themselves!

And if I wasn't mistaken, some of them were even laughing.

I slipped behind one of the three people surrounding Frank. She was a massive girl—at least six foot two, and solidly built. I slipped my foot between hers, and then shoved her hard. She tripped over my foot and went flying to the ground. Quick as a flash, I joined Frank in the middle of the circle. Back-to-back with him, I felt safer. There's no one I'd rather be in a fight with.

"What the heck is going on?" said Frank.

"I don't know!"

Two guys rushed us at once.

"Left!" I yelled, letting Frank know which way I was going to go. Right as the two guys were about to collide into us, I stepped wide to the left. Frank stepped to the right. They ran right past us, with too much momentum to slow down—until I grabbed one of them by his long ponytail, snapping his head back. He fell backward like a character from a cartoon, stiff as a board. When I looked up, Frank was tossing the other guy over his shoulder.

Somehow, Lenni appeared right next to us.

"Good job, guys! Glad to see you can handle yourselves."

A new, bigger circle had formed around us. It seemed to be the entire Krewe de Crude. They were breathing hard, and there were a lot of black eyes and spreading bruises. But there were still more than a dozen people surrounding us. These were not odds I liked.

Sybil stepped forward. Lenni must have gotten her pretty hard, because there was a small trickle of blood dripping out of her right nostril.

"You guys are pretty good," she said. Weirdly, she didn't seem angry. She sounded . . . impressed?

"Thanks," said Lenni, pretending to clean her nails on her shirt, although it was a toss-up as to which was dirtier. "You guys are pretty tight yourselves."

"So what are you really doing here? Sharkey knows we wouldn't deal in stolen stuff, not like that, anyway. Did he really send you?"

"No." I stepped forward. I had no idea who this Sharkey character was, but I was getting the sense that there was more to Sybil than met the eye. I was going to go out on a limb and try something.

"I'm Joe. This is my brother Frank."

Frank waved.

"We have family here in New Orleans, and last year, someone broke in and stole their stuff. Then they burned the house down. They lost everything. We're just trying to figure out what happened. Lenni was helping us because we didn't know who else to turn to."

At the mention of the fire, some of the Krewe nodded and exchanged looks. Sybil didn't say anything until I was done. Then she looked me up and down.

"We've heard about those jobs. That's not our style. We take from the rich, give to the poor. Like Robin Hood, you know? We started a soup kitchen in the neighborhood last year. We love New Orleans. It's our home. Those guys, they're just destroying things. Taking from anyone. I'd love to get my hands on them."

She pounded one fist into the palm of her other hand. With the look in her eyes, and the blood trickling down her nose, I wouldn't want to mess with her, even if she did weigh only a hundred pounds soaking wet.

The longer we talked, the calmer everyone became. A few drifted off to the other side of the warehouse. Sybil flopped back down on the couch. Lenni sat down heavily on the floor.

"I can tell you they're not anyone in the neighborhood," Sybil continued. "Whoever these freaks are, they're not operating out of the Bywater."

"Any clues on who they might be?" asked Lenni.

"I wish."

"Can you tell us anything that might help us find them?" said Frank.

"No. Wait, yes! I don't know how helpful this will be, but the stuff that they steal—none of it shows up in the pawnshops or thrift stores. I don't know what they're doing with it, but they're not selling it."

That was interesting. I had no idea what it might mean, but it was definitely out of the ordinary.

"If you find these guys, let me know. They're messing with my city—they're going to have to deal with me."

There were some shouts of agreement from the assembled Krewe. We hung out with them a little longer, and Sybil told us about all the projects they were doing in the neighborhood—the soup kitchen, a community garden, a local fashion line that taught kids how to sew and make their own clothes.

"Where does all the money come from?" asked Frank at one point. No one answered.

Lenni gave him a look and then poked him in the ribs. "Ignore him. He was dropped on his head as a kid."

Shortly after that, we left. As we walked back through the Bywater, I could tell Frank was still upset about something.

"Should we call the cops on them or something? Who knows where their money is coming from?"

Lenni hit him again. "Don't you fabulous spy boys have something better to do than harass people who are actually trying to make life better down here?"

She had a point. Frank blushed.

"You're right, I'm sorry."

"Of course I'm right," said Lenni. She looked at an imaginary watch on her arm. "Look at that, time for me to go. There's a second line tonight, and I don't want to miss it."

She pulled her skateboard out of her bag and hopped on it. Soon she was zooming off.

"Wait!" I yelled. "Where are you staying? How can we contact you?"

"I've still got your phone!" Lenni yelled as she disappeared around the corner, leaving Frank and me scratching our heads.

"What's a second line?" I asked Frank.

He shrugged.

With nothing else to do, we decided to follow our last remaining clue. The phone we'd followed to the Bywater belonged to one Andrew Richelieu. According to the police records, he was the spoiled son of a rich banking family and had had no idea his phone was even missing. Chances were, he wouldn't have much information for us, but we had to try.

I pulled out my phone and called the number the police had given us for Andrew.

"What?" a surly voice answered on the other end.

"Hi, is this Andrew Richelieu?" I said, surprised.

"Uh, duh."

"Well, this is Joe Hardy. I'm working with the New Orleans Police Department. I believe they mentioned I might be contacting you about—"

"Whatever. I don't really care, and I have a party tonight to get ready for. What do you want?"

Man, the police report had been kind! This guy was a brat.

"I'd like to talk to you about the theft of your phone."

"Fine. Party starts at eight p.m. Ask the butler to find me when you get here."

The line went dead. Andrew, it seemed, was a man of few words—and all of them were hostile.

Four hours later, Frank and I were seated in the back of a taxi, on our way up to the Garden District. Parties seemed to be the order of the day. The streets were lined with huge columned mansions, all of them lit up with tiki torches and mini spotlights, with parties that spilled out onto their lawns and balconies. Some were formal affairs—black ties and evening gowns, with elegantly simple masks. Others were wild, raging parties with dancing and blaring music. And the parties weren't contained to the houses. Every corner seemed to have an impromptu band performing, people dancing, laughing, singing.

I could really get to like this town, I thought.

Finally we arrived at Andrew's house. Unlike many of its neighbors, his house was clearly modern. It was made of glass and burnished bronze and looked like a tiny skyscraper, complete with a pointy tower on top. It was out of place on the street of old French houses, but somehow, it worked. Weird as it was, it was beautiful.

Much, much weirder than the house itself were the people. The costumes here were among the most extravagant we had seen yet. One man was wearing a suit made entirely of blue and red feathers, which extended from his body to impossible lengths, creating huge parrot wings and a long tail that trailed behind him. A woman was wearing what appeared to be a live ivy plant, growing out of a pot on the top of her head. There were animal masks that seemed to be grafted onto people's necks, making it look as though they really were half-man, half-animal.

"Wow," said Frank. "And I thought people went all out on Halloween in Bayport!"

We ducked past the revelers on the front lawn, who were all surrounding a giant sculpture that was made out of test tubes filled with various colored liquids. Every now and then, one of the partygoers would grab one and drink from it, but the stuff inside was sort of sludgy and odd, and not like any beverage I had ever seen before. It took twenty minutes to find the butler, and forty more for Andrew to come find us.

He was wearing a costume that seemed, at first, boring: a simple gray suit, nicely tailored. As he approached us, however, I realized I was wrong. The suit wasn't gray. It was brown. No, blue! Finally I realized that whatever the suit was made of, it was shifting colors as he walked, pulsating in time to his movements. It must have been unbelievably expensive.

"Aren't you a little young to be police?" said Andrew, before we had even introduced ourselves. In person, he was even ruder than on the phone. He had short spiky brown hair and a mouth fixed in a permanent sneer. He looked like the sort of kid who had been half bully, half coward. Also, there was no way he was that much older than I was.

"We're part of a special crimes unit," Frank said, trying to keep the anger out of his voice.

"It's about time the police department realized I'm an important person in this town, and sent some specialists in," sniffed Andrew. "Did you know that my father owns half the casinos in Louisiana?"

I took a deep breath and told myself to count to three before I answered. There was only one useful tack to take with someone like this.

"Of course, Mr. Richelieu. How could we not?"

This pleased Andrew, and his mouth twisted up into a sour smile.

"Now, about your stolen phone. Is there anything you can remember from that day?"

"Oh, who knows! I mean, I have six phones. Or maybe seven? I can never keep track of them anyway. Honestly, until the police called, I didn't even know it was missing."

Frank and I traded looks. Seven phones? What did he need that many gadgets for? Frank pressed him a little.

"Do you remember anything about when it disappeared? Where? If anyone strange was following you around?"

Andrew's eyes narrowed. "Look, I told you I don't know. Jeez. Shouldn't you be out solving crimes? Can't you, like, dust for DNA or something? Are we done yet?"

If he wasn't even going to try, there seemed to be little point in asking further questions. I gave him a card with my number on it, in case he remembered anything more. He turned away and dropped it on the ground before he'd gone two feet.

Our last clue had proven to be a dead end.

"Let's get out of here," I said to Frank. We turned to leave, and ended up getting completely lost inside the strange modernist architecture and the swirling party.

Somehow we ended up in a very long hallway—but every door was locked. We turned to go back the way we had come, only to find three costumed partyers blocking our way out. All three were wearing long robes in different colors, with simple silver masks.

"Frank and Joe Hardy," said one, in a deep, gruff voice. "Prepare to die!"

CHAPTER 9

NANCY

MADAME LEVEAUX KNOWS ALL

It was almost impossible for me to keep from laughing as Bess, George, and I advanced on Frank and Joe. The two of them had backed up against the wall and were crouched down in fighting stances.

"We don't want to hurt you," said Frank.

"Too bad," said George, in a fake, growly, baritone voice. "Because *we* want to hurt *you*."

"Bring it," said Joe. He waved us on with the tips of his fingers, like he was the hero in a martial arts movie.

Finally, when we were almost on top of them, I reached up and yanked off the mask.

"Nancy Drew!" yelled Frank. "What the heck?"

"What are you doing here?" said Joe. He was still in his crouching tiger position.

"Funny, I was about to ask you the same question," I said.

"Scaring the pants off you," said George.

"You got that right," said Bess. She crouched low in her robe, mimicking Joe. He hastily stood up as he realized that he and Frank weren't about to duel their way out of this hallway, and that he looked silly.

"Very funny," said Joe. "But really, what are you guys doing here?"

"It's a long story," I said. "Though something tells me you might already know parts of it."

I don't think it took the best detective in the world to figure out that the Hardy boys weren't just here for Mardi Gras. And my intuition told me that whatever they were working on, it was connected to Daniel's death. Why else would we have ended up at the same party?

Joe smiled. "We'll tell you our story if you tell us yours."

I laughed.

"We were just about to head out," Frank said. "Want to go somewhere and compare notes?"

"And get some food?" said George. "Did you see the food at this party? None of it was actually . . . food. It was all, like, foams and liquids in test tubes with labels that said 'pulled pork' and 'mac 'n' cheese.'"

"They tasted all right," said Bess. "If you ignored the texture issues."

"So that's what those tubes were!" said Joe. "We were wondering."

"I saw a diner not far from here," I said. I remembered noticing it through the window of the taxi as we came in. "It was kind of overflowing with people, but I think that's true for the entire city right now."

We decided to take our chances.

Bess, George, and I pulled our costumes off. Andrew, the host, had given them to us when we walked in, saying that the evening gowns Yvette had lent us "wouldn't do." We dropped them with the butler on our way out.

The party had been lame anyway. Aaron had been too busy talking with Andrew and all their other friends to spend much time with us—even with Bess. Everyone else seemed totally shallow and boring.

The diner was as packed as I remembered, but we spent the twenty-minute wait getting caught up. By unspoken agreement, we didn't mention our cases until we were seated at a table.

"What happened to your hair?" said Bess. "You guys trying a new look?"

"It's a disguise," Frank said quietly. "Undercover work."

"I kind of like it," I said. "Makes you both look edgy."

"Or totally ridiculous." George laughed.

Joe grinned. "We can do your hair next, George."

"No way!"

Finally, in a booth next to a group of people dressed as the characters from *The Wizard of Oz*, we got the chance to compare notes.

It took us all of about ten seconds of talking to realize that our cases were probably connected. Turned out that Daniel's warehouse was on the list of properties that the New Orleans Police Department had given to Frank and Joe as part of this gang's crime wave. They told us all about Lenni, and the Krewe de Crude, and the rest of their adventures.

I started to tell them about our investigations, when Joe suddenly snapped to attention and blurted out, "Oh my God!"

"What?" I said. We all tensed up. What had Joe realized? What important clue had we all missed?

"Did you see this on the menu? Tater tachos? They're like . . . nachos, but with Tater Tots. That's brilliant. This is the best city on Earth."

We all agreed that that was amazing, and ordered five of them. Then it was back to detective work.

"It doesn't sound like any of your gang would have been at Daniel's party," I said, when I'd finished recounting our experiences.

"No," Frank agreed. "But I wonder . . . Joe, what was it Sybil said about the stolen stuff?"

"That none of it was showing up on the black market."

"Right. If the gang was selling the stuff to someone directly, they wouldn't need a pawnshop or a fence."

"But that person would need to be pretty well off," said George.

"Like Aaron!" I said. Even after the rescue, I still didn't trust him 100 percent.

"Or Nicole," added Bess.

"Or Andrew," said Joe. "I mean, he certainly seemed rich."

"True, but he doesn't have any connection with Daniel."

"That we know of," Frank said. "Maybe it's time we did some more research on his phone. Even if he won't give us any more information, maybe it will."

"I've got some experience with bringing dead machines back to life," said George. "Want me to take a crack at it?"

"Sure," Frank said. "Why don't we go down to police headquarters tomorrow? We gave it back to their evidence room for safekeeping."

"While you guys are on that," added Joe, "Nancy and I can look into this Nicole Leveaux character, since she seems to be the one we know the least about."

"Sounds good," said Bess. "And I can do some more research on Aaron."

I turned and gave her a look.

"He asked me out again while we were at the party."

"You'll be our mole," I said. "Find out everything you can about him."

"On it," said Bess.

Right then, the tachos arrived.

"Wow," I said. "These are definitely the best things I have ever eaten."

"Especially after that space food at the party," George chimed in.

Detective work ceased while we devoured the food, which took all of about ten seconds.

Once the food was gone, we talked for a little while longer, but soon the excitement of the last few days started to catch up with all of us, and we were yawning into the remains of the tachos. We decided to meet up in the morning at the Hardys' hotel room and then go from there.

We showed up on the boys' doorstep bright and early the next morning. Frank answered almost as soon as we knocked.

"Nice digs!" said George, as she snagged a muffin off the complimentary tray that was sitting outside their room.

"You guys are fancy," I said, as I took in the room.

"It's all ATAC," said Frank.

"BLAARGH TREAACKLE ACK," said Joe into his pillow.

"I believe he said 'good morning,'" Frank translated for him. "Joe's not a morning person."

The four of us "encouraged" him to get up by throwing pillows at him. Once he was out of the shower, we worked up a plan.

"I never talked to Nicole at the party, but she may remember me, so I'll need a disguise," I explained. "Why don't we pretend to be visiting for Mardi Gras, and see if we can get her to talk? Maybe we can even pretend we're interested in buying property, or investing in her place, and see if she'll say anything useful."

"That's our plan?" said Joe.

"You got a better one?" I said.

"Okay, good point."

"I've already called down to the main store. She should be in today." Despite her strange appearance, everything I'd heard about her painted Nicole Leveaux as a savvy—and tireless—businesswoman. I wasn't surprised to hear she was working during Mardi Gras.

"While you guys are on that," said George, "Frank and I are going down to the New Orleans Police Department to see what other information we can coax out of Andrew's phone."

"And I'm going to meet Aaron for lunch in the Central Business District, right by where he works," Bess said. "Hopefully I can get him to take me back to his office, and I'll get a chance to root around in there."

"Man, you got the best job," said Joe.

"You should try being cuter." Bess winked at him.

After I borrowed a baseball cap from the boys and some big sunglasses from Bess, we were all piling into separate taxis.

Joe and I ended up at Nicole's flagship store: a giant, four-story Voodoo Emporium right near the levee of the Mississippi River. The place was filled with more souvenirs—and tourists—than I could ever have imagined.

"Who knew there were this many kinds of plastic spiders in the world?" said Joe, pointing to an entire wall filled with spiders in every size and color possible.

"Snakes, too," I said, pointing to another display.

We wandered through the floors, looking at the strange items on sale. They had everything from shrunken heads to life-size witches that came alive and cackled when you wandered near.

"This is the tackiest place I've ever been," said Joe.

"Oh," said a voice from behind us. "Are you looking for real magic?"

We turned and found ourselves face-to-face with Nicole. She seemed to have come out of nowhere. It was a little unnerving. She was wearing another crazy outfit. This time, it was a gold turban with a purple shawl and a wrap dress. She obviously believed in this voodoo stuff a little too much.

"Hi!" I said, in a peppy voice. "We were just browsing. We're here on vacation. My name's Cindy, and this is my boyfriend Alex."

"Really? Well, welcome to the Crescent City. As we say in New Orleans, *laissez les bons temps rouler*. What did you say your name was again?"

"Cindy."

"Well, Cindy, would you like to see some real magic?"

"Sure," I said, wondering how we were going to get some information out of her.

"Give me your hand."

Nicole held out her hand and I placed mine in it, palm up. She stared at it intently for a moment.

"I'm getting a vision. The spirits are communicating with me."

Nicole started taking in rapid, shallow breaths. Her eyes rolled back in her head. Her grip on my hand became tighter and tighter. It started to hurt. Her whole body started to shake. I looked at Joe. He shrugged, a worried frown on his face. This was getting scary.

Nicole uttered a low, soft moan. When she started talking, her voice was a raspy whisper.

"You are not who you say you are. Your name is Nancy Drew. You are a detective from River Heights."

I guess my disguise wasn't very good. I tried to pull my hand away, but her grip was like a vise.

"Your father is Carson Drew," she continued. "He

has interests here—a client. A dead client."

"How do you know all this?!"

Nicole stopped shaking. Her eyes came back into her sockets normally. But her grip on my hand didn't change.

"Because I'm not a fool," she said, her voice normal again. "You think I didn't clock you the moment you walked into my store? I have a photographic memory, girlie. Helped me go from being just another street fortune-teller to the owner of the biggest chain of souvenir shops in all of Louisiana. I saw you at Daniel's party, and when I heard who you were, I looked you up."

I had underestimated Nicole. She might look silly, but underneath her costumes was an impressive mind.

"Did your dad put you up to this? Or are you working on your own? I've read all about your impressive mystery solving. And you!"

Nicole turned on Joe.

"Who are you? Your face seems familiar. You and she have worked together in the past, haven't you? On a case involving that singer from the Royal We, and the mercenaries that were sent after her. What's your story?"

Yikes! The last thing I wanted to do was blow Joe's ATAC cover.

"He's just a friend. Really."

Nicole didn't look convinced. But she let go of my hand.

"Well, regardless, you don't have to come around here anymore. I'm no longer interested in Daniel's old warehouse."

This was news.

"What? Why?" said Joe.

"It no longer suits my needs. And as soon as I can get Aaron on the phone, I'm going to tell him that as well. Now if you'll excuse me, I have real customers to help."

It sounded a little fishy to me, but that was all Nicole was willing to say.

"Do you think she's telling the truth?" I asked Joe.

"Maybe. But it certainly sounds suspicious. Why would it suddenly not be suitable? She doesn't seem like the sort of person who would bid on a building before she was certain it was what she needed."

I had to agree. Nicole's strange behavior just added one more mystery to the mix.

CHAPTER **10**

FRANK

THE CASE HEATS UP!

Getting to the New Orleans Police Department central station took over an hour, thanks to the Mardi Gras celebrations.

"I think this is the first time I've been in a traffic jam caused by people dressed as Vegas showgirls—at ten in the morning!" said George, marveling at the people on the streets.

"Yeah," I agreed. "In Bayport, the showgirls don't usually block up traffic until noon."

She laughed. I liked George. She was one of the few girls I knew who didn't make me feel like a total geek all the time—maybe because she was just as much of a geek as I was.

"Before I forget, take this." I pulled a laminated

badge out of my backpack. It had a photo of George on it and said in big letters TECHNOLOGY CONSULTANT. There was no agency name on it—ATAC liked to keep a low profile—but if any police agency across the country scanned the badge, or called the number on the back, they would find that George now had higher security clearance than most police chiefs.

"What's this?" George asked as I passed it to her.

"It's your credentials. You'll need it to get into the evidence room at police headquarters."

"Cool!" said George. "Man, in River Heights all we've ever had to do to get access to police headquarters was sweet-talk Chief McGinnis."

We talked about the cases they'd worked on recently, and George told me all about the radio hookups and wireless microphones she'd built to help foil a pair of shoplifters. It wasn't often I got to geek out about spy stuff with someone my age who wasn't from ATAC.

"It's amazing how much you guys do!" I said admiringly. "I don't know if Joe and I would have been able to solve half your cases without ATAC's support."

"Flatterer," said George. "I'm sure you would have. You'd figure it out. You guys are pretty resourceful."

We traded stories until the taxi finally made it to the police station. The desk sergeant recognized me at the door. I guess they don't see that many teenagers with national security clearance. He raised an eyebrow at

George, but once he scanned her badge, he waved us both in.

"What do you guys need?" he asked.

"Andrew Richelieu's phone. And if you have it, a spare office with a big desk?"

"It's Mardi Gras," the desk sergeant grumbled. "Almost all the desks are empty, other than mine."

"Sorry, man," I said.

"So what's the story on this phone?" asked George, as we sat down in a bare office, home to a desk, two chairs, a single dead plant, and nothing else.

"It was stolen during a parade. Andrew didn't even notice it was gone until the police called him about it. Apparently, he's so rich, he has half a dozen different phones."

"And you guys got something off it?"

"It wouldn't power up when the police found it, but Joe managed to get it on. The only thing we found was a video, which led us to the Bywater, and a dead end. Here, I'll show you."

I powered up my laptop and played the video, which I'd copied off the phone just in case it stopped working entirely. Right as it finished, the desk sergeant appeared.

"One cellular phone, bagged and tagged. Make sure you put it back the way you found it." He handed us a plastic bag. Inside was Andrew's phone.

George took it out and began examining it. She weighed it carefully in her hand.

"It's superlight," she marveled. She looked at the make and model. She frowned. "Mind if I use the laptop for a second?"

"Go right ahead," I said, pushing it toward her.

She tapped on the keyboard and pulled up a search engine. After a few seconds, she was deep into the world of technology blogs.

"That's what I thought!" she exclaimed.

"What?"

"The phone is so light, and I didn't recognize the make or model. So I did a little searching—it's a beta version of a phone that won't even be on the market until next year. A few have surfaced on the Internet, and people have been blogging about them, but this is definitely something you can't get in stores. This thing is worth a small fortune. I'm surprised it survived being stolen and dropped, really. These beta version phones tend to be pretty flimsy."

"That explains why the thieves went out of their way to steal it. It breaks with their pattern, but they must have seen him using it and known what it was."

Already I was glad George was there. I fired up the phone and showed George how most of the menus were inaccessible. Together, we began working on it, connecting it to my laptop to try and bypass its broken operating system and get right at the data stored inside.

It was hours of painstaking work, trying different pathways, all of which ended unsuccessfully. But each time we came a little bit closer. Finally, after nearly four hours, we had a breakthrough.

"Got it!" I yelled excitedly. A bar popped up on the desktop, showing the download progress of Andrew's contacts, text messages, and recent calls. It was going v-e-r-y slowly. It would probably take at least an hour, and there was a good chance it would damage the phone's hard drive and wipe the information off it forever. But we had done it!

"High five," said George.

"Want to leave that downloading and grab some lunch?" I asked.

Before George could answer, the door burst open.

"Hey! You're working on those robbery/arson cases, right?" the desk sergeant asked breathlessly.

"Yes, why?" I said.

"Because we just got a call, and there's one going down right now! We've got a squad car and a fire engine on their way, but they're stuck in Mardi Gras traffic!"

George and I shot out of our chairs. We got the address of the call from the sergeant, grabbed my laptop, and ran out the door.

To save us time on the busy streets, the sergeant lent us two New Orleans Police Department bikes. It was much, much easier to navigate the busy streets full of partygoers, musicians, and performers on a bike than in a car. We went ten times faster than we had on our way to the station.

Finally we made it to the address we had been given, which turned out to be a small home in an area of town known as Tremé. It was right across the street from a large park.

The block was quiet, with only a few costumed revelers milling around on the street, the remains of a recent parade. There was no sign of a robbery, or of a fire.

"False alarm?" wondered George.

"I guess so," I agreed bitterly. This might have been our chance to catch them red-handed.

Suddenly the door to the house burst open, and a stream of masked men came bursting out. They all wore very traditional costumes, like jesters with long-nosed masks. There were at least a dozen of them. In their arms and on their backs they had bags loaded down with possessions from the house. Behind them, a wave of smoke poured out of the door.

"Stop!" I yelled. Fat chance. They streamed off in different directions, creating a chaotic swirl that had clearly been planned ahead of time.

I reached out and grabbed the arm of the nearest one. He yanked back, nearly pulling me off balance.

"Not so fast, buddy," yelled George, as she grabbed

him by the backpack. He pulled this way and that, but between the two of us, we had him firmly in hand.

I reached up to pull his mask off, and he head-butted his face directly into mine. The long beak nose of his mask slammed into my forehead. An inch to either side and he would have pecked out my eye. As it was, he managed to pull his arm out of my hand. He tried to run, but George still had a death grip on his bag. He fell backward to the ground.

Just then there was the sound of breaking glass from the house, and a scream. I looked up to see a small boy leaning out the window above the decorative balcony on the second floor.

"Help!" he screamed.

George and I hesitated, unsure of what to do. In that moment, the thief rolled away from us. I looked at George. We could still stop him—but who knew how long that kid had before the fire reached his room. Without a word, we both ran toward the house, hoping we weren't already too late!

HOT PURSUIT

On our way out of Nicole's Voodoo Emporium, Joe's phone rang. From the expression on his face, I could tell instantly it was important.

"That was the New Orleans Police Department," he said as he hung up. "There's a robbery in progress that matches the MO of our suspects!"

"Where is it?" I asked.

"Not far," said Joe, tapping away on his phone to pull up a map. "If we run, we might be able to get there in time to stop them."

He took off through the crowd of costumed people. Every block in the city was a never-ending maze of shifting human bodies. Beads rained down on us from above. Live music and giant speakers assaulted our ears.

I grabbed Joe's hand so we wouldn't be separated, and we wormed our way through the congested city.

"Look," said Joe, after about ten minutes. A plume of smoke was rising up from behind a house not far from where we stood.

"We're too late!" I said.

"Maybe not. Come on!"

We pushed harder, and finally popped out of the crowd of revelers onto a street that was relatively calm. Smoke was pouring from a small wooden house in the middle of the block, and the few people on the street were standing around staring. From inside, I heard a child scream.

"There's someone in there," I yelled.

We ran for the house. As we did, Frank and George burst through an upstairs window carrying two unconscious small children. They teetered on a decorative balcony that was barely big enough to hold them. It didn't look very strong to begin with. With the fire raging inside, who knew how much longer it would hold up?

"Stand still," yelled Joe. "We're coming."

We stood beneath the balcony. There was no way we could reach them, and it would be impossible for them to climb down while carrying those children. I had an idea.

"Joe, if I get on your shoulders, they can lower the kids down to me."

Joe squatted, and I swiftly climbed up his back and balanced carefully on top of him. One by one, George and Frank lowered the kids down to me, I passed them to one of the bystanders, and he set them on the ground. Once that was done, Frank and George climbed down quickly. Parts of the balcony were already beginning to collapse inward as they descended.

"What happened?" Joe asked. In the distance, we could hear the siren of an approaching fire truck.

Frank told us what we missed.

"They're gone now," said Joe. "Darn! If only we had gotten here sooner."

"We've still got a chance," said George. "Quick, Frank, hand me your computer."

Frank gave George a quizzical look, but he did as she asked.

"I slipped my cell phone into the pocket of the guy we tackled," she explained. She pulled up a map of New Orleans, with one glowing blue dot.

"There he is!" she said joyfully. "This will let us track him in real time—at least until he realizes what I did."

Firefighters were on the scene now. Two rushed over to the children.

"Things look to be in hand here," said Joe. "Let's go after the robbers before we lose them!"

"We'll never catch up with them on foot," I said.

"On it," said Frank. He spoke quickly into his phone.

"Lenni and the Krewe de Crude are nearby," he explained. "They said they'll bring us bikes we can use."

We waited five long minutes, watching the blue dot recede into the distance on the map. It was torture. Finally the Hardys' friends showed up with the bikes.

"What's going on?" asked Lenni, after Frank had introduced us.

"No time to lose! We'll explain on the way."

The Krewe members had to leave, but Lenni stayed with us. We all hopped onto the spare bikes. Each was cobbled together from lots of different bikes and they were as heavily decorated as many of the costumes I had seen. The bike I was on had a unicorn's head built between the handlebars, and a fake tail coming off the seat!

George tried to balance the laptop on her seat and pedal at the same time and nearly fell.

"Here, let me!" said Lenni. Somehow, she made biking while holding the computer look effortless.

Soon we were in hot pursuit of the little blue dot. On our bikes, we were able to catch up with it ever so slowly. Every time I managed to get next to Lenni, the blue light was a little closer.

Please, I said to myself, *don't let him find that phone!* It was our only link to these crimes. Any other clues they might have left behind were just ashes now.

"There he is!" shouted George suddenly. She pointed into the crowd ahead of us.

"Which one is he?" I yelled back.

"The one with the mask!"

"Which mask?" There were hundreds of masks out there!

"The weird beak-nosed one. In the dark purple outfit!"

I saw him. He was maybe two hundred yards away, in the thickest part of the crowd. We tried to ride our bikes into the street, but it was no use. We all hopped off and left them at the curb.

George led the way as we burrowed deeper into the mass of people. Feathers and fake fur brushed up against me at every turn. My toes were stepped on, my back was elbowed, but we were gaining on him.

"There he is," said Frank, spotting our quarry in the crowd again.

Unfortunately, it looked like he'd spotted us as well. He yelled something I couldn't hear, and suddenly the crowd around me erupted.

Hands were pushing me, hitting me, shoving me. Someone slammed Joe and me together, and my head started ringing from the impact. It was impossible to tell where all the blows were coming from, or who was doing it. The crowd must have been full of the rest of his gang.

"He's getting away down that alley!" I heard Frank yell. I stumbled toward his voice, just trying to stay on my feet. My impact with Joe must have been harder than I thought, because my nose was bleeding slightly. If this turned into a stampede, someone could easily be trampled to death.

Finally I broke free of the crowd and burst into a tiny alley. It was empty. I hoped it was the alley Frank had seen the guy go down. I raced to the end of it—only to find another huge crowd and no sign of our guy.

"Where is he?" Joe's voice came over my shoulder.

"I don't see him anywhere!"

We peered this way and that. Lenni, Frank, and George all caught up with us. None of us had escaped the crowd uninjured. Frank looked like he had the beginnings of a black eye, and George was half limping.

We searched the alley anxiously, looking for any place our costumed gang member might be hiding. Joe grabbed my shoulder and pointed to two large garbage cans halfway back up the alley.

Silently we approached them.

One . . . two . . . three, mouthed Joe.

On three, we simultaneously pulled the lids open to reveal . . . yesterday's trash.

"Over here," yelled Frank, back at the head of the alley. "I think I found him. Or at least, what's left of him."

In a small pile on the ground, underneath an empty plastic bag, lay the thief's mask and costume. George shoved her hand into one of the side pockets and pulled out her phone.

"Darn," she said. "I guess it was too much to hope he would somehow find it and decide to take it with him. We were so close!"

We stood dejectedly around, staring at the costume. I carefully used the plastic bag to pick it up.

"Maybe this will have some more information for us," I said. "And if there's anyone who can learn about a person from their clothes, it's Bess. We need to get this to her ASAP!"

"Let's get back on the bikes and get out of here," said Joe. "Maybe we can still catch up with them."

We hurried back through the alley and into the dense crowd. Even without a gang of masked men trying to slow us down, it was tough going. But finally we broke through to where we had left the bikes.

But they were gone. Someone must have stolen them in the few short minutes we'd left them unwatched— probably other members of the gang.

"Oh no," cried Lenni. "I left the laptop with the bikes!"

"That had all the information from Andrew's phone!" cried George. "Now we'll never know what was on there!"

Things had just gone from bad to worse.

CHAPTER **12**

JOE

A PICTURE IS WORTH A
THOUSAND WORDS

"I can't believe we lost those bikes," said Lenni, for probably the hundredth time.

"I told you," I said. "ATAC will pay to replace them."

"It's not the same," replied Lenni. "Your bike is like . . . part of you. They made those bikes out of pieces. Decorated them. Loved them! It's going to be hard to tell them we lost them. We owe them big-time."

"Sybil will understand," said Frank. "I mean, she wants these guys caught as badly as we do."

We all lapsed back into silence. We'd had to walk back and were almost at the hotel. With Mardi Gras in full swing, getting a cab was impossible. I wanted to be out among the costumed partyers, having fun and enjoying the music. Instead we were walking back home in silence, all of us caught up in our own little worlds. To have come so close to solving the case, to catching the criminals, and then have them slip right out of our hands—it was infuriating.

"Hey Bess." Nancy had finally managed to get Bess on her cell phone. That was another terrible thing about working this case during a party the size of Mardi Gras—all the cell phone circuits were constantly busy. Unless you were super lucky, it took twenty minutes to make a phone call.

"Something's come up. Can you break off your date early? Oh, great. Meet us at Frank and Joe's hotel." She shut her phone.

"What did Bess say?" I asked.

"Date's already over. She's on her way."

We walked along in silence again. We beat Bess to the hotel, but only by a few minutes. George and Frank hopped on the computer as soon as we made it back. Nancy paced. I sat on the couch and played catch with one of the cushions. As soon as Bess walked through the door, we pounced on her.

"What did you learn about Aaron?" Nancy asked.

"Look at this," I said, tossing the costume at her. She caught it reflexively, without even noticing me.

"What happened to you guys?" she asked. "You look beat!"

I forgot that we'd all been injured in the crowd. We probably looked a mess. No wonder we'd gotten so many odd looks on the way back.

Nancy explained everything. While she did, Bess absentmindedly examined the costume, feeling the fabric carefully with her fingers.

"Sounds like I missed out on all the adventure. What was the place that got hit, anyway?"

"Looks like it used to be a deli," answered George from the computer. "It closed down a few months ago. The family was living in an illegal apartment upstairs."

"Let's hope that explains why the gang didn't know they were there," added Frank. "This was the first time they hit somewhere while people were home. I'd hate for that to become their new pattern."

"It makes no sense," I said. "What are they getting out of this?" I punched the pillow in frustration.

"What about you? Learn anything about Aaron?" asked Nancy.

"Tons. But not applicable to the case. He took me to his office. See that building over there?" Bess pointed out the window to the one genuine skyscraper on the New Orleans skyline.

"His office is on, like, the nine hundredth floor of that building. It has an amazing view. Everything inside it is glass and light wood. Looks really Swedish. He showed me his plans for the city, and all the projects he's working on. He's a real workaholic. Plus, he likes to hear himself talk."

Bess paused for a moment and looked down at her hands, as though she had just realized what she was holding. "What's this, anyway?"

We explained where the costume had come from. Bess started to examine it more carefully.

"One thing I can tell you is that whoever owned this had money. This is expensive velvet, good dye job. The stitching? That's real gold thread. And all of this was done by hand. This is a one-of-a-kind, couture costume."

"Stolen," said Frank. "Must have been. Maybe from one of the earlier robberies?"

Bess shook her head. "Not possible. See these tears here in the fabric? Someone pulled this costume off in a hurry. But it fit them perfectly. If this wasn't tailored to them, there would be lots of places where it didn't fit right, and the seams would have burst all over. Whoever was wearing this had it made for them."

"It fits with what Sybil told us," I said. "They're not in this for the money. Nicole's got cash—and her store was full of costumes."

"Yeah, but those costumes were cheap, mass-produced things," said Nancy. "Aaron's pretty well off too. Both of them wanted to buy Daniel's property, and they were there when he was killed."

"But none of this really connects them with all the attacks," I added.

"There is one rich kid who we know has good taste in costumes," said George, from over at the computer. "And whose cell phone is already connected to the crimes."

"Andrew!" we all burst out.

"Bingo," said George. "And though he might not be connected to Daniel, you'd be amazed what else he is connected with. Drunk and disorderly charges, public nuisance, vandalism. The guy's got a rap sheet of minor crimes a mile long."

"How do you know that?" said Nancy, amazed.

"The Louisiana Department of Justice keeps very thorough, web-accessible records." George smiled. "Want to see his mug shot?"

"What if his phone wasn't stolen?" I said. "What if he's part of the gang, and he dropped it, and made up that cover story when the police showed up?"

"It would explain why he never reported it stolen!" said Frank.

"It would also mean he was a lot smarter than I would have guessed," muttered Nancy under her breath. We all laughed.

"Sounds like we need some proof," I said. "And since Andrew isn't likely to give it to us, that means a little reconnaissance—the kind best done at night."

I smiled. There had been far too little spy stuff on this case so far.

"Bess, can you call Aaron?" said Nancy. "Tell him I thought Andrew was cute, and see if he can arrange a triple date for us, with someone for George."

"Ugh," said George. "Make that a double date. I'll help you guys with Andrew. Do you have any wireless cameras? Remember the recent case we told you about, where we used a mic setup? If I can wire the two of you up, I can work from this end and look up anything you might find."

"Good idea," said Frank. "You can also help us out with any security he might have. We've got a wireless camera in our standard ATAC kit."

In short order, plans were made with Aaron to ensure that Andrew would be out of his house tonight. So long as Frank and I avoided the butler, we'd be able to look around for a while.

With our plans set, all that was left to do was wait. Nancy and Bess went to get ready for their "dates." An hour after they left, we got a text from Nancy asking us to join them later—that was the signal we had pre-arranged to let us know that Andrew was with them. The coast was clear.

Joe and I dressed in all black, including special black gloves and masks that ATAC had given us. On a normal night, we might have stood out, but this was Mardi

Gras, and no one paid us any attention on the street.

Andrew's house looked different with the lights off and the gates closed. It looked scary, like something out of a horror movie, but it also looked like the butler and any other servants were out. In fact, the whole block seemed quiet tonight. Apparently, the parties were somewhere else this evening.

We circled the house. The fence extended around it in all directions, ten feet high and topped with spikes. And were those . . .

"Look," I said to Frank, careful to point only with my eyes. Casually, Frank turned his head.

"Motion detectors," he said.

"That's what I thought," I said.

"I see them," said George through my earpiece. "Joe, can you turn so I can get a look at the front door? Most security companies put up stickers there. It'll give us an idea of what we're dealing with."

"On it," I replied. I was glad we had her with us.

"Okay, got it," said George. "Give me a few minutes." The microphone went quiet.

Around the back of the house we found a big backyard. Thankfully, one corner of it was overgrown with cypress trees. They would provide us some cover for climbing. And there was a set of patio doors that should be easy to jimmy open. Now if George could take care of the cameras, we'd be set.

"All right, it's a LockJaw system," said George. "This will be easy. Do you know where you'll be coming in?"

"The backyard," I whispered.

"Are you guys in position?"

"Yes."

"Okay. On the count of five, the cameras are going to go down for twenty seconds due to a localized power outage. Any longer than that and the alarms go off automatically, so move fast."

I counted down under my breath. Right on five, the little red dots on the cameras went out, and they stopped swiveling on their bases.

"Go!" I said to Frank. "We've got twenty seconds."

Twenty, nineteen, eighteen . . . I counted in my head.

We raced to the cover of the trees and threw ourselves on the fence. We were up and over in record time, racing for the house.

Thirteen, twelve, eleven . . .

That was when the dogs hit us.

They came streaking out of nowhere, two all-black Doberman pinschers. They opened their mouths to bark, but no sound came out. They must have had their voice boxes removed, something people frequently did when they had dogs that were meant not to just scare people away—but to hurt them.

I pushed a button on the base of my glove. I could feel the sudden tingle in my hands as they powered up, just in time. One of the dogs jumped at me. I ducked and swatted it on its side. A blue spark leaped from my hand. The dog whined once, and then passed out. The Taser had worked perfectly. The dog was down, but breathing. A few feet away, I saw Frank do the same. They'd wake up in two hours with a slight bruise.

Five, four, three . . .

We made it to the patio, and I already knew we were too late. We had three seconds to get the lock open before the motion sensors turned on and the alarms went off. There was no way we could pick a lock in that time.

Thankfully, we didn't have to. Frank grabbed the door—and it slid right open. We slipped inside and closed it behind us, right as the detectors came back to life.

"Best security systems in the world are useless if you don't remember to lock the doors," whispered George in my ear, her laughter barely contained.

The house was dark on the inside. We slipped on our masks. In the hole where the eye should be was a care-fully constructed infrared lens, made out of a flexible plastic. With the masks on, the inside of the house was lit with a dim red light.

"According to his contract with LockJaw, there are no detectors within the house. Looks like anyone who works for him has the night off for Mardi Gras. So get to it!" said George.

We didn't need any more encouragement. We started at the bottom of the house and planned to work our way up, but we didn't even have to.

The fourth door we opened was clearly an office of some kind. Or really, a trophy room. The walls were covered with photos—Andrew with a gun standing over a dead deer. Andrew with his arm around various beautiful women. Andrew shaking the hand of Louisiana's governor.

And there, on one whole wall, were photos of buildings on fire.

"Are you getting this?" I asked George.

"Already matching them up with the police files. Those are our robberies. Good job, guys!"

Andrew was our man. Or at least, one of them.

CHAPTER 13

KNOCKING THE CASE OUT

At any moment I thought I might scream. Never had I been so horribly tortured. It just went on and on and on.

"And then, remember that time in 2007? All the monkeys? That was the best ball ever."

Andrew droned on and on about Mardi Gras parties and costumes and insane cakes and famous guests. It was like listening to the gossip column in some local newspaper being read on repeat. And we were only on our appetizers. At least the restaurant we were at was nice. It was a weird old barbecue joint way out in the middle of nowhere. It was named, appropriately enough, the Joint. And the food was good.

Aaron wasn't much help. He and Bess were chatting

quietly with each other on the other side of the table, leaving me stranded with Andrew, who seemed to assume that I liked the sound of his voice as much as he obviously did.

I stared at my fork, idly wondering if I could somehow stab myself accidentally and get to go to the hospital.

"I said, don't you just love the Royal We?"

I snapped to attention. For once, Andrew was actually asking me a question!

"Yeah, I—"

"Right? They're great. They played at my birthday last year."

I thought about telling him I knew Kijani, the lead singer of the Royal We. But I doubted he would even notice I was still talking.

I knew this was important, that by getting Andrew out of his house we were helping to solve the case, but man, would I much rather have been the one breaking in!

"Aaron throws the best parties, of course. Don't you, Aaron? He even threw a huge party immediately after Katrina. There can be no excuse, he says, for canceling a party. Right?"

Aaron shrugged. "Please, you flatter me. I try to make my own little additions to the social calendar of the city, that's all."

"You'll be coming to his ball tomorrow, of course," Andrew said to Bess and me. "Aaron's providing all the costumes! He won't tell us what the theme is. It's unheard of. Who knows what he'll have us dressed up as? Buildings, probably. My outfit better fit right, that's all I'm saying."

Finally I couldn't take it anymore. Andrew took a deep breath, probably to complain again, and I saw my chance.

"So, Aaron," I said, cutting Andrew off and leaning across the table. "Bess tells me you have big plans for New Orleans?"

Aaron smiled. "Yes!" he said. "I've always loved this city, but it's stuck in the past. It needs to join the twenty-first century. And I am just the person to bring it there. I have a ten-year plan to put this city on the map, architecturally. To make it a . . . a shining beacon for modern architecture!"

"You must be excited at the possibility of having Daniel's place to work on."

"The sadness of his death makes excitement seem wrong. But it will be the first property I work on that I own outright," he responded. "So I am excited. If I get it."

"Since Nicole dropped out of the bidding, I can't see how you wouldn't get it. You're the only serious offer out there!"

"Nicole what?"

"She dropped out. I mean, that's what she told me."

"You were talking with her?"

"Yeah," I said. This was not where I wanted the conversation to go. The last thing I wanted was to tip off Andrew to the investigation. "Just helping my dad out some."

"Nancy has a way of ferreting out information," said Bess. "She's got quite the reputation for crime solving back in River Heights."

Was I mistaken, or did Andrew twitch when Bess mentioned crimes?

"Interesting," said Aaron. His eyes had a faraway look in them, as though he was looking right through me. He shook his head and snapped back to attention.

"I didn't know that. I guess this is a celebratory dinner, then!" He raised his glass in a toast. "To the future of New Orleans."

We clinked glasses. I did my best to keep him on the topic of the city, which was infinitely more interesting than hearing about Andrew's outfit at his twenty-first birthday party. I could sense Andrew pouting next to me, but I ignored him as best I could.

Halfway through dinner, a text arrived from Joe.

"Keep them there! On our way!"

A tingle went through my spine. If they were headed to the restaurant, it could mean only one thing:

They'd found some evidence linking Andrew to the crimes. He would be in custody before the night was over.

If I could put up with him for that long. I tuned back into the conversation in time to hear Andrew describe the haircut he was going to get for the party tomorrow, which was like his haircut now, but shorter. But not too much shorter. Just a little bit shorter.

I leaned across the table to Bess.

"I think Frank, Joe, and George might be dropping by for dessert," I whispered.

Bess smiled. She knew what that meant. "Awesome!"

Ten minutes later, the door to the Joint swung open, and in they walked. Andrew shut up immediately.

"What are you doing here?" he said, standing up from the table.

"Andrew Richelieu? We have reason to believe that you've been involved with the robbery and arson of thirteen different properties in the city. We've notified the police, and they will be at your house with a search warrant by the time you get home," said Joe, with obvious relish.

"What? This is ridiculous. I'm calling my lawyer."

"I wouldn't do that if I were you," said Frank. "If you cooperate, and give us the names of the other people involved, we are willing to offer you a deal."

"Aaron, help me out here," said Andrew, looking desperate. "This is preposterous."

They must have found proof! This was great. We'd have this case wrapped up by tomorrow.

"Aaron," said Bess. "Talk to him. Tell him to come clean. Frank and Joe are friends of ours—they'll help him."

Aaron stood up. His wolf-yellow eyes turned cold.

"Andrew, they've got you. You should do the right thing. Turn yourself in. You need help. Trust me."

Andrew flushed with rage. "What? How dare you!"

With no warning, he flung himself across the table at Aaron. The two of them went down in a heap. The table was smashed. The dishes went flying. A waiter came running out of the kitchen, took one look at the scene, and ran back inside.

Andrew had his hands around Aaron's throat. Bess and I rushed over to pull Andrew off him, but before we could, Aaron rolled over and slammed Andrew to the ground.

By the time we separated them, Andrew was unconscious.

I checked his pulse. It was weak. I slapped his cheek, but he didn't respond.

"Get an ambulance!" I yelled. "He's unconscious."

Dark black and blue marks were already rising on Aaron's neck, and he seemed to be having trouble breathing. They both needed medical attention, now.

It took long minutes before the ambulance finally arrived. Aaron waved them away, saying he was fine, and insisted that they take Andrew to the hospital first.

Frank and Joe tried to get into the ambulance with Andrew, but the emergency medical technicians forbade it.

"Police and family only, I'm afraid," said one. The Hardys' ATAC badges might get them a lot of places, but it wasn't going to work here.

"Take my car," said Aaron, holding up the keys. "I'll get a cab. Go!"

"Thank you," said Frank.

"I'll make sure he gets home safely," said Bess. "Nancy, you go with them."

I was torn. I didn't want Bess to be alone. But I wanted to hear more about what had happened. And if Andrew woke up, I wanted to be there for it.

"I'll go with them, Nance," added George. "You go with Frank and Joe."

That decided it. We hopped in the car and raced to the hospital.

The emergency room was filled with party-related injuries. Bloodstained costumes and broken masks were everywhere. It looked like a massacre at a circus. If I hadn't been so focused on Andrew, I would have been terrified.

"We're here to see Andrew Richelieu," Joe said at the desk.

"Hold on a moment," said the woman behind the desk. She picked up the phone. "Yes, sir," she said. "The kids you said would be coming are here."

On the other side of the room, a man in a three-piece gray pinstripe suit snapped a cell phone shut and strode over. He looked like he was wearing the costume of a businessman from the 1940s. But it didn't look like a costume on him!

"Nancy Drew, Frank Hardy, and Joe Hardy, I presume?" he said.

We nodded.

"I am Lawrence Worthington III, the Richelieu family lawyer. Aaron Pexa phoned me and told me what happened. My client, Andrew Richelieu, is in a coma, no thanks to any of you."

"Wait a second," said Frank. "That wasn't our fault."

"Fault is an issue for a judge to decide," said the lawyer. "But as of right now, I have a temporary restraining order on the three of you. None of you is to be within two hundred feet of Andrew or his property."

Joe and Frank looked ready to argue with the lawyer, but there really wasn't anything they could do.

"And I've already spoken with the police—the chief is an old friend—and there will be no search. Pleasure doing business with you boys. I assume we're done now. Good evening."

Lawrence Worthington III tipped his hat at us and walked out.

Our criminal was in a coma. Our chance of getting evidence was gone. And now we couldn't go near him again!

This case was back at the beginning again.

CHAPTER **14**

F R A N K

MURDERED? OR MURDERER?

This was probably the hardest Joe and I had ever worked on a case to get exactly nowhere. We knew Andrew was involved—but we couldn't touch him. And since he was in a coma, we couldn't even work out a deal. We contacted ATAC and had them speak to Andrew's parents, but they wouldn't budge on the restraining order.

And to top it all off, Mom was about to kill us. We'd bumped into her and Dad by accident on the street outside the hotel. Until then, we'd managed to see them only on purpose, when Joe and I had time to carefully hide our hair under wigs and hats. But today we'd run straight into them on our way to Nancy's place.

"I know it's all fun and games, and you got caught

up in the Mardi Gras spirit, but look at yourselves!" she said, pointing at our hair. The many Mardi Gras beads around her neck rustled when she moved. "How are you going to go back to school looking like that?"

"We can dye it back," said Joe.

"Or shave our heads," I added.

"Or wear hats?" said Dad. At least he knew why we had done it, though he couldn't say anything.

"You're not helping," said Mom, giving him a dirty look. She threw her hands up at the sky. "Fine! Look like crazy people. What do I care? I'm just your mother."

I couldn't help but laugh. The tension was broken. Now we wouldn't have to bother with the stupid wigs anymore.

"We're late for a lunch date," said Dad.

"Your father has kept me on a whirlwind tour of the city. It's been so romantic. I'm sorry we haven't been spending much time with you boys."

We assured them it was fine—with a wink for Dad—and hurried off on our way.

"So what did Nancy tell us?" Joe asked.

"That the party was pretty full that night, but she was sure there had to be a guest list somewhere. So that's a place to start."

With our case dead in the water, we'd decided to help Nancy on hers. There was still a chance they were connected, but it was beginning to look less and less likely. Seemed like Daniel was just unlucky enough to have his building burned down by one person, and then get murdered by someone else. Some people just couldn't catch a break.

When we arrived at the late Daniel's house, I gave a low whistle. This place was swank. Nancy answered the door on the first knock.

"Where is everybody?" I asked. The place sounded empty.

"Dad's been working out of Daniel's office. He says being here makes him sad. Yvette, Daniel's sister, felt the same way, so she's gotten a hotel room downtown. She says she's going to sell the place after we leave."

"Hey, Frank! Hey, Joe!" Bess called from the kitchen. "Come grab some pancakes before George scarfs them all down."

"No need to tell me twice," said Joe.

Over some lopsided—but delicious—pancakes, we discussed the status of Nancy's case.

"So it seems like the arson and the murder aren't related," said George.

"Probably not," said Nancy. "But who knows?"

"Right. But for the moment, since we've got no leads on the arson, let's look at it as a separate case," I added.

"What we know is this," said Nancy. She pulled out a big piece of paper and put it in the middle of the table. Bess and Joe moved the dishes out of the way so we could all lean over it. George had her laptop set up in front of her and was typing away.

"Daniel was involved in negotiations with two people over his building: Nicole Leveaux and Aaron Pexa."

She drew all three names on the paper, with lines connecting them.

"They were both at the party that night. Since then, Nicole's been acting suspicious. She's dropped out of the bidding on the building."

"Maybe she wanted to throw off suspicion," I said. "Or felt bad about killing Daniel. It could have been an accident."

"What if Daniel told her he was going to sell to Aaron?" added Bess. "Maybe she got so angry, she choked him without realizing what she was doing."

"All possible," said Nancy, writing down the various reasons. "But on the other hand, Aaron is the one buying the building in the end—so maybe he got exactly what he wanted, and just had to take Daniel out to do it."

"That's not her name!" George suddenly shouted.

"What?" we all asked at the same time.

"Nicole Leveaux. It's not even her real name. I was suspicious about that—turns out her real name is Nicole Pasulka, and she's from Chicago. She changed it when she moved down here."

"Can you search and see if she's got a criminal record

under that name? And check Aaron, too, while you're at it."

We chowed down on the last of the pancakes while George did some searching.

"Aaron's clean. But looks like Nicole was wanted for a bunch of misdemeanors—fraud, bad checks, that kind of stuff."

"Well, that's enough to move her to the top of our list," I said. "I think it's time we went and talked to her again."

"Agreed," said Nancy.

"Why doesn't someone else go this time?" said Joe. "She didn't seem to like me much, and I promised Lenni I'd go with her to explain the bikes to the Krewe. Plus, I figured I'd take a picture of Andrew along and see if anyone recognizes him. Maybe they can fill us in on some of his accomplices."

"And Bess and I told Aaron we'd drop by his office," said George. "He needs some help setting up for the party, and he promised me he'd show me the 3D printers they use in his office to construct models. They can actually make figures you design on the computer in real life!"

"Sounds like a plan. Should we meet back here before his party?" Nancy asked.

"If we're done in time," said Bess. "Or else we'll just see you there."

With everything agreed, we split up.

Nancy and I headed out to Nicole's house, which was thankfully located not far from Daniel's. We walked through a crowded parade. From a float in front of us, massive speakers blasted techno, and dancers dressed like underwater creatures threw beads into the crowds. Everyone looked so happy.

"When this case is done, I hope we have time to enjoy Mardi Gras a little," said Nancy.

"That's exactly what I was thinking."

We smiled at each other. It was nice having Nancy around—someone else who could understand what it was like being in ATAC.

Nicole's house was one of the old New Orleans–style houses, which meant that there was just a small gate on the street, which led back to a large courtyard.

"Look at this," Nancy said, pointing to a sign on the gate.

HOLD ALL MAIL AT POST OFFICE, it read.

"And look at that," I whispered. I pointed toward the house. It was set back, and there were a lot of plants on the porch. All the shutters were closed, and the lights were off. But one of the shutters right by the front door looked as though it had been broken, and it banged back and forth in the wind.

I had a bad feeling about this. We pushed the main buzzer. Off in the distance, we heard a chime go off. But no one answered. We tried again. Nothing.

"Should we . . . ," I started to ask, but Nancy already had a set of lock picks out of her bag.

It took only a moment to open the gate. Nicole's security system was nothing like Andrew's. I was a little nervous, considering how our last breaking-and-entering experience had gone, but I had to admit, I was worried.

"What if someone's broken in?" said Nancy. "We have to check this out."

Up close, the house seemed even more deserted. Nothing moved in the courtyard. Aside from the one broken shutter, everything else was closed and boarded up.

Nancy touched the door, and it swung open. This was getting weirder and weirder.

She put her finger to her lips, and quietly, we both went inside.

The house was eerily quiet. The power must have been off, I realized, and without the usual hum of a thousand electronic gadgets, it seemed like the inside of a tomb. We wandered from room to room but saw no one. Even though the shutters were closed, thankfully light still filtered in through the slats, or else it would have been pitch-black inside.

In one or two rooms, it was obvious someone had left in a hurry. A hall closet was in disarray, as though someone had pulled a few things out of it and just let the rest lay where they had fallen. Inside the kitchen, two drawers were opened and empty.

"She's gone," I said. My voice sounded incredibly loud in the empty house. No point in being quiet if there was no one around to hear us.

Nancy sighed.

"Yup," she agreed. "How much you want to bet she's somewhere in South America or another country where we can't bring her back for a murder trial?"

Before I could answer her, a noise came from above us. In a normal house, it would have gone completely unnoticed—it sounded like something small being dropped on a carpeted floor, right above our heads. Nancy and I froze.

I jerked my head back the way we had come. There were stairs near the main entrance. We crept quietly and quickly back. Were we lucky enough to have caught Nicole in the act of leaving?

At the top of the stairs, I hesitated. The hallway spread in three directions: right, left, and center. I was pretty sure the sound had come from the left, but who knew which door led to the right room? This place was big.

With nothing else to do, I listened for a minute. There—I thought I caught the sound of footsteps coming from behind the door to the right.

I opened the door to reveal a long hallway, with a bright red carpet, multiple doors on either side, Mardi Gras masks hanging from all the walls—and two masked men, dressed like jesters, holding guns.

"Run, Nancy!" I yelled.

The gunmen seemed as surprised to see us as we were to see them. It gave us a crucial one-second head start. I pushed backward, knocking Nancy out of the way as I pulled the door shut. The door shuddered as a bullet struck it.

Whoever these guys were, they were serious.

"Ooph!" Nancy said, as she hit the ground hard. I reached down to help her up, and the door flew open, knocking me over and back toward the stairs.

Nancy kicked out, getting the first gunman right in the knee. He landed next to me and his gun went flying down to the first floor. I threw myself on top of him. He rolled, and we were teetering at the top step. If we went down like this, we'd probably both break our necks!

I heard the sound of fighting, but I couldn't pull my attention away for one second to see if Nancy was okay. This guy was strong! We grappled on the floor, each trying to get the upper hand and send the other over the steps.

I heard heavy breathing, and sounds of struggle. Nancy was holding her own.

I got the guy on his back and managed to pin one of his arms with one of my legs. Now I had the advantage. Slowly, I pushed him toward the top step.

"Frank! Watch out!"

Something hit me hard in the back. I fell to the left,

and just had time to crunch into a ball before I started rolling down the steps. I hit the ground and kept rolling, hoping that the other gunman wasn't a good shot. It was only as I stood up that I realized what had hit me: Nancy. She was on her back at the bottom of the stairs. I looked up, and the gunmen were gone.

CHAPTER 15

THIS PARTY IS THE BOMB

"Are you all right?"

I came to and found Frank standing above me. It took me a moment to remember where we were.

"The gunmen! Frank, watch out!" The last thing I remembered was being sent tumbling down the steps, which meant those goons were still up there. At any moment, I expected bullets to come flying down.

"They're gone," said Frank. "They took off running down the hallway."

I noticed something in my hand. I was holding the other thief's gun. Between that, and the one on the ground not far from us, I realized we must have disarmed them.

"We've got their guns," I said. "Let's go after them."

We emptied the two guns of bullets and took them with us. We didn't want to accidentally shoot anybody, but it might help to intimidate them. We stalked our way through the rooms upstairs, but the men were nowhere to be found. Unfortunately, we found a servant's staircase that led to a back door, which stood open. The two men were gone.

"Who do you think they were?" I wondered.

"The costumes—they looked sort of like the ones the gang was wearing when George and I ran into them. But I guess all black costumes look pretty similar. . . ."

"Do you think they were working with Nicole? Or for her?" Could she be the woman behind the gang?

"Maybe," said Frank. "Or they could have been looking for her. Maybe someone sent them to get Nicole out of the way."

"But why?" I wondered. "She's already dropped out of the bidding on Daniel's warehouse."

"Let's see if they left anything behind up here."

We started working our way slowly through the second floor of the house again. Here, there was more evidence of disarray. The doors and drawers in her bedroom were flung open, clothes strewn everywhere.

"Someone left here in a hurry," I said.

"Or those two guys were looking for something," said Frank.

Every piece of evidence seemed to point in both

directions: Nicole was innocent, she was guilty; she was in danger, she was dangerous.

Finally we made our way to what must have been her office. The room was paneled in dark wood, with velvet drapes. All the walls were lined with bookshelves, and there was a ladder going up one wall. It was like a miniature library, complete with a giant oak desk with one of those brass-and-green-glass lamps. Like her bedroom, the room had obviously been gone through by someone in a hurry.

"This is going to take awhile," I said, pointing to the massive filing cabinets in the corner of the room. There must have been reams and reams of files in them.

"At least no one set the evidence on fire this time," Frank joked.

"That's looking on the bright side," I muttered, as I pulled open one of the desk drawers to reveal folder after folder of papers. Each was carefully labeled. Unfortunately, the labels were either in some language I'd never heard of, or some kind of complicated code. They didn't even seem to be organized alphabetically.

"This mean anything to you?" I asked Frank, showing him one of the labels.

"It means I need to study more languages, I think," he responded.

I decided to start with the folders that were lying on top of her desk. If we were lucky, they were out for a reason. I flipped open the first one. It was full of inventory lists. From the items described (200 plastic alligators, 100 rubber zombies), I guessed they were for Nicole's stores.

The next folder was receipts—food mostly, and toiletries. The next was just a list of music. But on the fourth, I got lucky.

The file was brimming with real estate notices, mostly for buildings up for sale, or recently purchased, all around New Orleans. Looked like Nicole was hoping to expand her empire, or at least keeping track of the possibilities. It was the first clipping that really got my attention.

"Hey, Frank, look who it is."

I held up the cutting from the *Times-Picayune*, which showed Aaron Pexa shaking hands with some city council member, standing in front of the burned-out shell of a building. The article hailed Aaron as a "native son of the Crescent City," who was doing his "civic duty" by promising to restore the charred remains to their former glory.

"Am I being overly suspicious, or do you want to bet that building is one of the ones the gang burned down?" I asked Frank.

"No need to bet," he replied. "I've got the list right here."

He took out his phone and pulled up a notepad application.

"There it is," he said. "Fourth on the list. The former home of Gisela's Hair Salon. What else is in the file?"

I began to read the addresses off the purchasing notices for different buildings. By the time we got to the fifth, Frank stopped checking. No doubt about it—they were all the buildings that had been destroyed.

"So Nicole's been keeping records on your fires," I began.

"And she had a reason to off Daniel," Frank finished my thought.

"But none of these list her as the buyer." I riffled through the file. "In fact, her name isn't mentioned anywhere on them."

"Do you think it's just a coincidence? That seems pretty far-fetched."

"No, but what if she's some sort of amateur detective? I mean, as someone who owned a lot of property in the city, she did have a reason to want these guys stopped."

"So you think those two guys were trying to . . . what? Kill her before she found out about them?"

"Maybe. Or maybe she controls the gang? I just don't know, Frank. Either way, she's not here."

We'd gone from not enough evidence to far too much. Neither was helping us make heads or tails of this case.

I used my phone to take photos of all the relevant

real estate clippings, while Frank called ATAC. He'd have them watch for her name—both her names—on any bus, plane, or train headed out of the state.

We continued searching her office, but found nothing. Slowly it grew darker inside. The mountain of papers in Nicole's office seemed undiminished. We kept our ears open, but if anyone returned to the house, they did it in total silence. Finally it was too dark to see in the office.

"The last thing I want to do is go to this party," said Frank, staring up from the pile of files he had assembled around him.

"I'm with you," I agreed. "But we told Joe, George, and Bess we'd meet them there. Maybe one of them found something useful."

We spent a few minutes putting things back as best we could, although since we couldn't understand Nicole's filing system, we probably made a mess of it. Then we headed out to Aaron's house.

The house couldn't have been more out of place. On a block full of Victorian mansions and old-school New Orleans houses, Aaron's house was a gorgeous glass box. The walls covered his property entirely, all the way up to the sidewalk. But he still had a lawn—it was just under glass. It looked like a giant aquarium, designed for people.

The party was set to start at eight p.m., and though

we showed up at eight thirty, we were still clearly early. The house was quiet when the butler opened the glass door.

"Ah, Ms. Drew and Mr. Hardy," the butler said in a cold voice. "Mr. Pexa warned us you would be early. You are to join your friends in his office." He sniffed loudly and stared sideways at our outfits. It was clear we were not dressed to his standards. I wanted to explain that we weren't early—we were, in fact, late—but it didn't seem worth it.

Frank rolled his eyes at the butler's back, and I had to stifle a laugh as we followed him up to Aaron's office.

"Nancy," said Aaron, as he sprang to his feet. He kissed me on the cheek. He seemed incredibly excited, probably because his party was about to start.

"And Joe," he said, grabbing Frank's hand and shaking it vigorously.

"Frank," Frank corrected. Aaron smiled as though he hadn't quite heard him properly.

"Whatever," Aaron said, his smile never leaving his face. "Come in, have a seat!"

"Hey y'all," said Bess, with a fake Southern drawl. "Take a load off."

"You sound more cowboy than Southern belle," said George, laughing. Everyone seemed to be having a great time.

"How was the party setup?"

"Great!" said Bess. "There was nothing for us to do. Aaron told us all about the parties he's thrown in the past."

"It sounds like tonight is going to be amazing," added George. "If his previous parties are anything to go by."

"You girls flatter me," said Aaron. He paused for a second. "No, I deserve it."

We all laughed.

"Now, the party will be starting momentarily, so here." He handed large packages to each of us. "Frank, we should leave the girls to get dressed in private. You can use the bathroom in the master bedroom. I'll show you where it is." He and Frank left the office.

The packages were heavy, and covered in silver paper. Bess tore into hers in record time.

"I've been so curious!" she said.

She pulled out a long, simple black robe. It was floor length, long-sleeved, and hooded. It had a mask that went with it, made of silver, with black material that went over your head at the back. George and I opened our packages to reveal identical outfits. Once they were on, no one would be able to tell us apart!

"Well, this is interesting," said Bess, though she sounded doubtful. "But I was expecting a little more. I wonder if everyone will have the same robe."

"The masks are strangely heavy," said George. "And look, they have little plugs at the back!"

"There is a matching socket on the robes," I said. "It looks like there's more to this outfit than meets the eye!"

Bess pulled hers on. She had a little trouble fitting the plugs into the socket, but once she did, we all gasped. The material of the robe had slowly begun to light up, a spreading pattern of silver that moved as she moved.

Bess saw her reflection in the window and clapped her hands. "Fantastic!" she yelled.

I turned and began to pull mine on when something caught my eye. Aaron's office, like the rest of his house, was a lot of glass. The pieces of glass that faced the inside of the house were one way, so we could see out, but no one could see in. Above his desk was a giant map of New Orleans, blocking out all the different properties he was working on.

Something about the map nagged at me as I got dressed. It looked familiar somehow. As I plugged the mask into the robe, it clicked.

The addresses were the same as the ones in Nicole's file! Each of the properties Aaron was working on had been burned to the ground by the mysterious gang. It all came together for me then. The arson wasn't to cover the robberies—the robberies were an excuse for the arson! That was why none of the stuff ended up on the black market. No one really cared about the thefts.

What connected all the crimes wasn't the places

they were before the fires, but what was going to be built there afterward. And Aaron had been smart—I imagined that most of those buildings were owned by friends of his, like Andrew, or people he did business with. That way his name wouldn't connect them all, unless you knew to look deeper. Aaron was at the heart of all of it. By burning down the properties he wanted to develop, he could buy them for a song!

"Bess! George!" I yelled. My brain was flying. Had Nicole figured this out? Where was she? Had Aaron killed her? Were we next? I had to tell them what I had figured out, but first we had to find Frank and get out of here.

But before I could say anything, two more masked figures entered the room. I reached up to pull my mask off, when Frank's voice came from the masked figure on the left.

"Don't!" he yelled. I paused.

"Frank! We have to get out of here. Aaron is the one—"

The other masked figure began laughing. It was Aaron, of course.

"I knew it was only a matter of time before you figured me out. I would have run yesterday, when you accused that fool, Andrew. But I had some business interests to take care of. I'd hate to escape the country only to find myself broke, you know. And besides, the masses of New Orleans were waiting for my party. I hate to disappoint my public. And believe me, this party is going to be a blast."

Bess and George were frozen. I realized they had no idea what was happening.

"His properties!" I said. "He's developing all the burned-down buildings into new places."

"That's not very important now, Nancy," Aaron said, his voice sickly sweet. "You want me to go over my crimes, one by one, so you can mark them all down? That's not going to happen. What's going to happen is this: I hear my guests arriving so I'm going to go downstairs, have a great party with my friends, and then get on a plane. And you're not going to do anything about it."

"Fat chance," said Bess.

"If you think that's happening, you really don't know Nancy," said George. "Or Frank."

Aaron laughed again.

"Those lovely light-up robes you're wearing? They're my special design. The power centers at the back of the neck? They're rigged to explode if you take them off. Or wander outside my house. Right now, there's an entire ballroom filled with living, dancing bombs. Tell them the truth, and they'll panic. Half of them will be pulling their masks off while the other half runs out the door. And when they all explode, it'll be your fault."

I had no idea if Aaron was telling the truth. But the

only way to find out was potentially fatal. He continued talking as he paced around the room.

"Anything that scares my guests—like the police showing up—might terrify someone into removing their mask, and you wouldn't want that, would you? Now, I'm being a terrible host. So I'm going to go downstairs and dance. Have a wonderful evening. I'll send you a postcard from somewhere tropical when I get there."

And with that, Aaron slipped out the door.

CHAPTER **16**

JOE

TO THE RES-KREWE!

"So you don't recognize him?" I asked, for what felt like the thirtieth time.

The guy in front of me shook his head. His gigantic, floppy mustache waggled around his face like a pair of fins. It was hard to take him seriously.

"Sorry, man," he said. "I ain't seen him."

Lenni and I had been showing pictures of Andrew all around the Bywater, hoping to find someone who knew him and might be able to identify his accomplices. So far, we'd turned up nothing.

This guy was the last one hanging out in the Krewe de Crude warehouse. I hadn't had much hope, but I figured we had to talk to everyone, just in case. What if the one person I didn't ask was the one who knew something?

"Any luck?" asked Lenni, as she zoomed past on a borrowed unicycle.

"No," I replied. "Where did you learn to do that?" She was awesome on anything with wheels!

"Just picked it up. That girl over on the couch showed me how. She didn't know Andrew either. I think we've struck out. I told you, these kids wouldn't deal with a guy like Andrew."

My phone rang while Lenni was chatting. It was Frank—right on time for me to tell him that we had found out exactly zero. I hoped he had better news.

"Joe! We're in trouble," Frank said as soon as I answered the phone. As he explained the situation, my jaw dropped. Man, he wasn't kidding!

"Joe?" asked Lenni, watching my facial expression. "Earth to Joe? Yo, Joe! You're scaring me, man. What's going on? Joe!?"

Frank hung up, and I turned to Lenni.

"They're in trouble. Aaron has taken his whole party hostage. They can't call the police—they need backup." I explained the situation to her.

"Backup?" said Lenni. "Like, say, a crew of bike punks who can show up and just look like part of the party?"

She gestured around us.

Brilliant! I thought.

I hopped up on a nearby table.

"Hey! HEY! Everyone!"

A few people looked up, but most of them continued with what they were doing. There went my brilliant backup posse plan.

Then Sybil stood up.

"HEY! Listen up," she said. She didn't scream, she was just loud enough for everyone in the warehouse to hear her. But still, everyone snapped to attention.

"Thanks," I said. Sybil nodded and gestured for me to continue. It felt a little bit like I was in a scene from *The Godfather*! But everyone was quiet, so I took a breath and went for it.

"So, you know those guys I've been asking about? The ones who've been burning down the city?"

"Yeah!" came a yell from the audience. "They suck!"

"Well, they've got my friends—and a whole lot of other people—held hostage in a building in the French Quarter. Most of the people don't even know what's going on, they just think it's a normal party. But if the police show up, they're going to kill everyone."

The crowd grew quiet. It was a tense, scary quiet.

"They need backup. They need people who can help them out, without tipping off their captors. They need a gang that can look like a normal Mardi Gras krewe. They need you!"

It seemed like no one was breathing. Then Sybil stood up.

"You heard him! Our city needs us. They've tried to burn us out! Are we going to sit by and let these guys get away with it?"

"NO!" the Krewe roared.

"Then saddle up!" Sibyl yelled back.

Suddenly the room was a flurry of noise and action. People were pulling on costumes and hopping on bikes. In under five minutes, I suddenly had twenty angry costumed punks at my disposal.

"Here," Sybil said, "hop on with me." She was wearing a fox mask and tail. On anyone else, it would have looked cute. On her, it looked cute—and dangerous.

Her bike was a monster of a bike. The tires and the lower frame were normal, but the handlebars and the seat were ten feet up in the air! It was like a giraffe bicycle. It also had a second seat behind the first one.

"You can get up on my shoulders," she said, squatting down. I'd never ridden a bike like this. I climbed up on her back, and then scrambled up on the rear seat while she held the bike steady. She hopped up on a table, then hopped up again onto the front seat. The bike wobbled for a second, but it stayed upright. I looked down at Lenni.

"I've got my board," said Lenni, "so I'm good! Let's go."

"Open the gates!" yelled Sybil. A large gate on one side of the warehouse began to roll upward. It must have once been the entrance for trucks, when this was a working factory. Now it served as a launching point for a tiny bike army.

Sybil rode at the front of the pack, her tall bike like the prow of a ship, cutting through the water. The streets were packed with Mari Gras parades and partyers, but they parted for the Krewe de Crude like a hot knife going through butter. They even applauded as we went past, mistaking us for just another street parade. Little did they know that the lives of a lot of people were depending on us.

Riding behind Sybil was terrifying. The bike shook with the wind, and I had no handle bars to hang on to—and no control over which way the bike went. I just balanced on the seat and hoped. It was kind of . . . exciting.

"WOOO-HOOO!" I yelled, as we pedaled into the night. I felt like a cowboy, riding off to save the town.

A chorus of yips and howls echoed from behind me. I looked back and caught sight of the entire Krewe de Crude. They rode on bikes of every shape and size: from super-tall ones like Sybil's, to ones where the riders were so low they were almost lying on their backs, the pedals far in front of them. Some of them rode on tandem bikes, where two people pedaled together on one extra-long bike. There were two other skateboarders aside from Lenni, and one dude on Rollerblades.

As I watched, a tourist with a camera the size of his

head tripped over the curb while trying to get a picture of the Krewe. He fell straight in front of the Rollerblader, who leaped effortlessly over him, landing two feet away from him on the other side. The guy didn't even blink! They were total pros.

Which was good, because we were going to need some coolheaded, able-bodied people on our side. A gang of arsonists and murderers. Bombs wired to blow. No way to tell our friends from our enemies.

I had to hand it to the city: New Orleans did it big.

CHAPTER 17

NANCY

ALL DRESSED UP AND READY TO BLOW!

"Just get here as soon as you can," said Frank over the phone to Joe. "And if you happen to have an army on you—who won't alarm the partygoers—bring them along."

He hung up. I realized we were all standing there frozen, afraid that at any moment we might spontaneously blow up. I took a deep breath, steadied my nerves, and took a step toward Frank.

When nothing happened, I breathed a sigh of relief. At least we could move around.

"Do you think Aaron's telling the truth?" I asked.

"No way to know," said Frank. "So we'd better assume so."

George—or was it Bess?—began feeling around the back of her mask.

"There's definitely something there," she said. It was George. "Nancy, come here."

I walked over to George and turned around so she could examine the back of my mask more closely.

"It looks like more than just a power source for the robe," she said. "But I couldn't say for sure what it is. I think I'd have to take it apart. And that might end poorly for all of us."

Frank joined her. "What do you think this is?" he said, poking softly at the back of my head.

"Looks like copper," said George. "Maybe that's the detonator?"

"Could be. Or the top of the battery for it."

"Right. Look at this piece, here. See how it runs all the way around?" George's finger traced a path along the back of my head. I was beginning to feel like a monkey having lice picked off its head at the zoo. Explosive lice!

"I think this is an antenna," said George excitedly.

"Totally," agreed Frank. "That's probably what he's using to blow them remotely. I wonder what frequency it's broadcasting on."

Antennas reminded me of our last case—and of the surveillance help George had given Frank and Joe earlier. An idea began forming in my head.

"Frank, do you have that remote camera you used when you broke into Andrew's house?" I asked.

"It might be in my pocket. I think Joe gave it back to me."

"Do you think you and George could use it to deactivate the detonators?"

"It's worth a shot," said George.

"It could work. We'd just have to figure out how he's broadcasting, and find a way to block the signal. It wouldn't get rid of the bombs, but it should make it impossible to set them off."

Frank hurried into the next room, and came back holding his jeans in one hand and a small camera, the size of a button, in the other.

"Got it," he said. He and George ran over to Aaron's desk. George began tapping away at his computer.

"I know a lot about radio transmitters and wireless networks," said George, "but zero about bombs."

"Thankfully, ATAC considers bombs a critical part of a good spy's education. Go to this Web page." Frank rattled off a long web address.

Bess sat down heavily on the couch.

"I can't believe I trusted him!" she said.

"We all did," I told her. "He rescued me, remember? This isn't your fault."

"Oh, Nancy, I feel terrible!"

"It's going to be all right. I'm going to go check on the party. Stay here."

I walked out into the hallway. It wasn't hard to find my way to the main ballroom—I just followed the sounds of music, and laughter, and dancing. At the center of the house was a huge room, which extended all the way to the roof of the building, making the entire ceiling one giant skylight. I found myself on a balcony two floors up, looking down on a crowd of a hundred costumed partyers. They were dancing, chatting, and admiring the decor. Not one of them was aware just how much danger they were in. I tried to pick out Aaron, but everyone looked the same. It was useless.

A spiral staircase led from the balcony down to the party below. I walked down, hoping that up close something might tip me off to Aaron's presence. But it was even more impossible to tell people apart than from a distance. It was just a sea of sparkling black robes and silver masks. I wandered into the crowd, and as I did, a disturbance began in the party. A few people were looking around quizzically, tapping at the sides of their masks. I sucked in a quick, fear-filled breath, but thankfully no one tried to remove their masks. Aaron must have given them instructions to keep them on.

"If we move the *BZZZZZ* . . . and attach . . ."

Out of nowhere, I heard George's voice in my ear. I

spun around, but she was nowhere to be found. Then I realized the voice was coming from all around me.

The antenna! They might not have been able to deactivate the bombs, but they had definitely hacked into the system. As I listened, George's and Frank's voices began broadcasting from every mask in the room. It gave me hope. I decided to head back upstairs and see if they were any closer to a solution.

I slipped among the confused, masked revelers and headed back toward the spiral staircase. As I did, a small masked figure stomped past me. Wherever the person was going, he or she was headed there in a hurry. The figure nearly knocked into me.

It was only as the crowd swallowed the figure up behind me that I realized something: I couldn't hear George and Frank coming from that person's mask! Which meant they didn't have an antenna. Which meant they weren't wired to explode. Which meant it was one of Aaron's gang!

I turned back to find the person, but he or she was already gone. But still, now we had a way to tell people apart. If George and Frank could neutralize these booby-trapped masks, we might have a chance.

I hiked up my robe and ran up the stairs, taking them two at a time. When I burst through Aaron's office door, everyone froze.

"It's me!" I said. "Whatever you're doing, it's working—

I can hear you guys broadcasting over all the antennas in all the masks."

"Yes!" said masked-Frank, giving masked-George a high five.

"It gets better," I said. "One person's mask wasn't broadcasting. If they don't have an antenna, they don't have a bomb, and they must be part of Aaron's gang. So if we can hijack the antennas, we can keep the bombs from going off and use them to tell people apart."

"We're on it," said George.

"You better hurry, though. The guy who passed me without an antenna seemed upset. They may be realizing that something is going on."

"Got it!" said Frank. "The motion sensors and the remote access on the detonators should be deactivated."

"So it's safe?" I asked.

"Yes," said Frank. "Well, probably. We're working on the fly with a system I've never used before. I think we've hacked it, but there's no way to know without trying."

We all stood still, four identically dressed figures in a crazy glass house. I knew what I had to do.

I grabbed my mask with both hands and yanked it off. I heard a sudden loud noise. Bess screamed.

JOE

CRASHING THE PARTY

"Yo, Frank, what's the situation?"

I could hear Bess screaming in the background. Things didn't sound good.

"You just nearly gave Bess a heart attack," Frank responded. "We were pretty sure we managed to deactivate the bombs, and just as Nancy tested the theory by removing her mask, my cell phone rang. We thought she was dead."

"My bad," I said. "But hey! No one's dead, right? Me and the Krewe de Crude are a block away from Aaron's house. What's up?"

"We've shut the bombs off, so we should be safe. But we don't want Aaron and his crew to know it until we're in place to take them all down. So we're staying robed up. We need half of you to surround the house and make sure no one gets away. Once they're in place, send everyone else in."

In the distance, the lit-up glass box of Aaron's house grew nearer and brighter.

"Can do," I said. "But how are we going to tell everyone apart?"

"That's the great part. Aaron's bombs are run by remote antennas. We've hijacked the system. Let us know when you're ready, and we'll start broadcasting. Anyone whose mask doesn't make noise? Take them down."

"Got it!"

I relayed to Sybil what Frank had told me. She took her hands off the handlebars (scaring the pants off me), put her pinkies in her mouth, and emitted the loudest whistle I'd ever heard. As one, the Krewe pulled their bikes in tight around her. Sybil explained the situation. As we approached the building, she started giving orders.

"Everyone on my right," she said. "Your job is to surround the building. If they're not broadcasting, don't let anyone get away. If you're on my left, you're going in with us."

The air was split by the sound of yips and howls, as the bikes, blades, and boards of the Krewe de Crude began to circle the house. We waited until everyone was in place, then I called Frank again.

"We're ready," I said.

"Welcome to the party," he said.

Sybil and I hopped off our bike. Lenni fell in right next to us. Behind us were fifteen or so costumed Krewe members. We threw open the door and walked right past the startled butler, who tried to stop us with cries of "Wait. Stop! Where are your invitations?"

One of the Krewe stopped, turned, and farted at him. "There's my invitation, man," he said. I guess they weren't called the Krewe de Crude for nothing.

We ran into the main ballroom, and I could finally see what Frank had been explaining. Everyone looked exactly the same. Tall or short, they were all wearing these weird, black, glowing robes. They looked like some really freaked-out cult. The few nearest the entrance stared at us, confused by our sudden appearance and our different costumes.

Right on cue, as we stepped into the main hall, the music changed. Aaron had been pumping some pop dance music in through hidden speakers, but that was suddenly replaced by the "Ode to Joy" broadcasting out of tiny, tinny speakers in each person's mask.

"What's this?" asked Lenni, when the music started.

"Beethoven," I replied. "It's Frank's ring tone on his phone."

Suddenly I noticed someone trying to slip deeper into the crowd. It was hard to be sure, but I didn't think there was any sound coming from the person's mask. I headed toward him, and he started running.

I tackled him in a flying leap. He went down, taking some other guests with him. But I was right! There was no music coming from his mask. He tried to get up, but Sybil knocked him on the head with a platter of food from one of the tables.

"Get 'em, boys!" she yelled. The Krewe exploded into the crowd. I expected people to take off running in fear, but I'd forgotten: This was New Orleans, a rough-and-tumble city that loved fighting as much as it did partying. In just a few seconds, the crowd had become a giant free-for-all, ten times worse than what we had gone through at the Krewe de Crude warehouse.

I saw Lenni get jumped by two robed figures and go down in a heap. Another Krewe de Crude member leaped in on top of the pile. One of the skateboarders was on his board, chasing someone down a staircase. Somewhere in this mess were Frank, Nancy, Bess, and George, but since I had no way of telling who they were, I concentrated on looking for someone else I knew was in here—Aaron.

Some guests were making for the exit at the back of the ballroom. One caught my eye. He was notice-ably taller than most of the other people around him. I wormed my way past groups of fighting people. Some-one grabbed my ankle, and I nearly went down, but

I managed to shake him off. I caught up with the tall masked figure right before the exit.

He wasn't broadcasting. I grabbed him by the sleeve— and he turned around and punched me in the face!

I heard a *crack* as he hit my nose. That was going to hurt in the morning, I was sure. But with all the adrenaline of the brawl rushing through my system, I barely felt it. I kicked him in the knee, and he fell. But as he did, he grabbed the top of my Mohawk, pulling me down with him.

We grappled on the floor, rolling this way and that, knocking into guests and tables full of food. Someone stomped on the masked man's hand, and he howled. While he was distracted, I yanked his mask off. It was Aaron!

He shoved me off him and tried to run, but his robe had gotten tangled around his feet while we wrestled. He tripped, and slammed headfirst into the wall. He went down in a half-conscious heap.

I turned and looked at the raging party/fight behind me. I'd never considered how I was going to get the Krewe de Crude to stop. . . .

"And then one guy came up behind me, and I thought for sure I was going down," I said. "But Bess jumped on his back! He ran around trying to get her off him, like a chicken with its head cut off!"

We were all safely back at the hotel, catching up on what had happened. After I caught Aaron, the fight slowly died down. One by one, his gang of thieves was captured. From what I heard, his guests thought it was the "most epic party ever." Even though Aaron was going to jail, it would be a long time before anyone threw a party as unique as that one.

I'd had to go to the hospital to have my nose looked at, but apparently, it wasn't broken. It just hurt a lot, and looked like I'd tried to open a door with it. I was icing it now, as we sat up on our private roof patio and watched the parade below.

"How many were there in the end?" asked George.

"The police said they arrested sixteen people in connection with the fires," I said. "And get this—they were all rich kids from good families! Aaron convinced them that they could get even richer if they went along with his plan. By burning down those buildings, they could buy them for a song, and then have Aaron redevelop them."

"Right," said Nancy. "So when Aaron finally had the money to buy one of them on his own, and Daniel refused to sell it to him, he went crazy and strangled him to death."

"Ugh." Bess shivered. "And to think I went on a date with him!"

"Two dates," teased George. Bess threw a set of

Mardi Gras beads at her, and George laughed. "He was charming, though. It's not all your fault."

I laughed, but it made my nose hurt. "Apparently, he had a private helicopter waiting for him at the levee," I added. "He was going to ditch the rest of his gang at the party. No honor among thieves . . ."

"So what happened with Nicole?" Nancy asked. "I hope she's all right."

"ATAC called me while we were at the hospital. They found her in Chicago. She'd gone home. When she had a meeting with Aaron, she saw that map and figured out the same thing you did—I guess it's that photographic memory she has. She put together that folder we found, just to make sure she was right. Then she fled town. When you mentioned that she was dropping her bid on the building, Aaron figured she'd found him out, and sent those two guys to kill her!"

It had been a crazy few days. But we still had two more nights left in our hotel room. And Nancy's dad was staying down to help Yvette settle her brother's estate. Which meant one thing.

"We have one more mystery to solve, guys," I said.

Everyone stopped dead.

After a moment of silence, Nancy asked, "What?"

"Where to get the best gumbo!"

"Yes!" yelled George. "That's a case I like the sound of."

CAROLYN KEENE
NANCY DREW

Secret Sabotage

Serial Sabotage

Sabotage Surrender

Secret Identity

Identity Theft

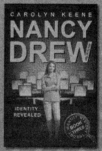

Identity Revealed

Model Crime

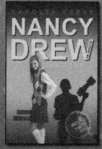

Model Menace

Model Suspect

INVESTIGATE THESE THREE THRILLING MYSTERY TRILOGIES!

Available wherever books are sold!
Aladdin • Simon & Schuster Children's Publishing • KIDS.SimonandSchuster.com

FRANKLIN W. DIXON

THE HARDY BOYS

Undercover Brothers®

INVESTIGATE THESE TWO ADVENTUROUS MYSTERY TRILOGIES WITH AGENTS FRANK AND JOE HARDY!

#28 Galaxy X

#29 X-plosion!

#31 Killer Mission

#32 Private Killer

#30 The X-Factor

#33 Killer Connections

From Aladdin
Published by Simon & Schuster

DID YOU LOVE THIS BOOK?

Simon & Schuster

IN THE

bookloop

Join *In the Book Loop* on Everloop.
Find more book lovers online and
read for FREE!

Log on to everloop.com
to join now!

everloop™
Our site. Our stuff. Our world.
www.everloop.com

No Chickens
Allowed.